On November 18, 1905, Lizzie got off the streetcar as usual, surrounded by several of her girlfriends from work. Within the protection of the group, Lizzie was laughing and chatting, her stalker temporarily forgotten. Then Lizzie saw Robhaut leaning against a nearby wall. She froze, and the chatter of the group died as the girls turned to follow her gaze. Lizzie held up a hand as if to ward off Robhaut's manic stare, and stammered that he still had a peace bond against him. Things happened very quickly after that. The sight of sweet Lizzie, who had rejected him, sent Robhaut into a highspeed come-apart. Gripping the handle of a knife, he seethed with resentment and rage. Suddenly Robhaut broke away from lounging against the storefront and rushed at Lizzie, who started to shriek. She didn't even have time to plead for her life—all she could do was scream. Her cries of terror were drowned in blood as Robhaut plunged the knife into her chest. She staggered back, but he followed, stabbing her three more times. She fell to the sidewalk, her bodice soaked in scarlet, her life draining away as she hit the ground. Robhaut spared the object of his obsession just one more glance. Then he pulled out a revolver, shoved the stubby barrel into his mouth, and squeezed the trigger, blowing the back of his skull off. His body collapsed on top of Lizzie's; he was dead before he landed. A murder-suicide, out in the open on a public street, is a surefire recipe for a haunting. Ever since the tragedy, Lizzie Kaussehull has haunted the corner of Lincoln and Carmen in Chicago. The streetcar Lizzie stepped down from on that fateful day is long gone, but the ghost of the pretty young murder victim remains. On nights when a full moon paints the sky with silver, Lizzie can still be heard. For her shrieking cries that echo into eternity, she has earned a nickname. Locals know her, appropriately, as Screaming Lizzie.

First Edition

GRAVE DEEDS
AND
DEAD PLOTS

by Sylvia Shults

For all the victims.

Introduction

Ask any paranormal investigator—or anyone interested in the supernatural, for that matter—what causes a place to be haunted? And you're going to get several variations on a theme. Unfinished business? Sure. A spirit attracted to a place they were familiar with in life? Of course.

A spirit hanging around the place they were murdered? Abso-freaking-lutely.

It's an unfortunate fact of the paranormal that some—not all, but some—hauntings are the result of violence. That includes the violence that people do to each other. Sometimes this is an accident, a life taken in the heat of the moment.

Others are the result of weeks or months of careful planning. There are predators out there who kill simply for the sake of killing. As unfathomable as it is to the rest of us, they enjoy it.

All of these deaths leave their mark on the places where they happened. Sometimes, the stain is subtle ... a window opens or closes on its own, a shadow drifts along a hallway. Other times, the violence echoes through the years—a woman's scream splits the night, a ghostly car slows, stops to drop off its ghastly cargo, the splash of a dead body hitting cold river water startles passersby.

Come with me as we explore these cases: true crime stories with the added frisson of a ghost story.

The Manhattan Well Murder (1799)

Gulielma Sands, known as Elma, lived in a boarding house in New York City. In December 1799, she was in a relationship with another tenant, a carpenter named Levi Weeks. The couple made plans to elope on December 22.

Around 8 pm that evening, Elma's cousin, Catherine Ring, heard the front door open and close. She smiled to herself, assuming it was Elma sneaking out to meet Levi. But Levi showed up at 10 pm demanding to know where Elma was. This unexpected development led to a search of the neighborhood.

Witnesses saw Elma in Lispenard's Meadow, a nearby lover's lane of sorts, walking with two unidentified men. Lispenard's Meadow was also the site of the Manhattan Well. On January 2, Elma's body was pulled from the well. She'd been dumped there, her neck broken.

The identities of the two men were never discovered. For lack of any other suspects, Levi Weeks was accused of Elma's murder. His wealthy oldest brother Ezra hired the best lawyers in town: Alexander Hamilton and Aaron Burr. The two-day trial was the first recorded murder trial in American history.

The case was expected to be a slam-dunk for the prosecution. Levi Weeks was in a relationship with Elma, and he was the last person to actually be seen with her. There were rumors (untrue) that Elma was pregnant, which seemed to give Levi motive for her murder.

But Hamilton and Burr knew their business. They cast serious reasonable doubt on the case, painting Elma as a loose woman, addicted to laudanum. Any guy could have killed her, they said. After only five minutes of deliberation, the jury found Levi Weeks not guilty.

Not that it did him any good. Weeks was so hated after the trial, he had to leave town. And Catherine Ring, Elma's cousin, had a few tart words for Alexander Hamilton.

"If thee dies a natural death, I shall think there is no justice in heaven!"

Catherine's curse backsplashed on pretty much everyone involved in the trial. Hamilton was killed in 1804, in a duel with his former partner, Aaron Burr. The judge in the trial simply disappeared after leaving his hotel one night. And Burr was loathed for killing Hamilton, tried for treason in 1807, lost his beloved daughter Theodosia to shipwreck in 1812, and died broke in 1836, the same day his divorce was finalized.

In 1817, houses were built in Lispenard's Meadow. The Manhattan Well ended up hidden in the basement of a four-story building at 129 Spring Street. The upper-middle-class home eventually became commercial property. In 1954, the building was purchased by the DaGrossa family, who opened a restaurant called Manhattan Bistro. By 1980, Manhattan Bistro had grown so much that they needed more storage. They excavated the cellar, and exposed the well that had been buried for nearly 200 years.

The discovery of the well seems to have kicked off the paranormal activity in the building. Since then, the spirit of Elma Sands has made her presence known. Witnesses have heard her screaming for her life, and have seen the apparition of a young woman, soaking wet, dressed in 18th-century clothing.

Restaurant manager Thomas King had many paranormal experiences during his time at the Bistro. One evening, he went down to the basement to get a bottle of wine from the large cage where the liquor was stored. He unlocked the gate, leaving the key in the lock, and went to the back wall for the bottle. When he turned around, he found the gate locked behind him, trapping him in the cage. The keys had been removed from the lock and placed on a box just out of reach. King was down there for an hour before other employees realized he was missing and came downstairs to rescue him. Manhattan Bistro went out of business in 2013. In 2014, the building was gutted, renovated, and became an upscale clothing boutique. The well was preserved, and is now in the corner of the men's department.

The Haunted Crossroads (1805)

Crossroads have traditionally been considered strange places. Musicians in search of demonically-bestowed talent hang around dark and deserted intersections, and in Great Britain, there was a tradition of burying criminals and suicides at crossroads. The reasons for this have been lost to folklore. Some say that crossroads represent a location "between worlds", which also makes then perfect places to summon demons. Others, focusing more on the ghostly than the demonic, theorize that having a place with four choices of direction would confuse the ghost of the person buried there, so it wouldn't be able to escape and go around haunting other places.

Some magistrates went even further in their sentencing when they condemned someone to hang, and used a crossroad as the scene of a grisly object lesson. When a criminal was executed, judges would sometimes include gibbeting in their sentence. The criminal's body would, after execution, be put into an iron cage, hung from a post, and left there to rot. Crossroads, again, were a popular choice for this display, because the corpse would be visible to people coming from four directions.

There is a crossroads just outside a town in England called Saxilby, near Lincoln, that was the scene of just such a punishment. The roads to Daddington and Harby cross there. It's not much to look at, mostly pavement, trees, and untidy weeds sprawled in the ditches. But for over four decades in the early nineteenth century, this was the final resting place of Tom Otter.

And nothing about it was ever remotely restful.

In 1805, a tall, handsome man came to Lincoln looking for

work as a laborer. Tom Temporal was quite the womanizer—he started seeing a young woman, and got her pregnant. Mary Kirkham was 24, and Tom was 28.

Mary went to court and petitioned the magistrates for child support. This was exactly what was allowed by the poor laws of the time. But these judges went a step further. They offered Tom a choice: marry the girl, or go to jail. Tom chose the bonds of holy matrimony, and on Sunday, November 3, 1805, Tom and Mary were escorted by the parish constables to the church in South Hykeham. Not the stuff romances are made of, but the couple was hitched.

But there was a problem—a big one. And a little one too. Namely, Tom's wife and infant daughter. See, Tom Temporal was not, as he claimed, a widower. Nor was he actually Tom Temporal—Temporal was his mother's maiden name. He was actually Tom Otter, and he had married Martha Rawlinson in Nottinghamshire on November 22, 1804, and she gave birth to their daughter just a month later.

Okay, let's do a bit of math here. Tom gets married November 1804 to Martha, who's eight months pregnant. Then about a year later, he marries Mary, who is—surprise!—also eight months pregnant. This means Tom ditched Martha pretty quickly after tying the knot, then legged it to London and got Mary pregnant around March of the very next year. What a prince. Tom was definitely a "love 'em and leave 'em" type of guy, but this time, it bit him in the ass.

On the evening of their wedding, Tom and Mary were traveling from South Hykeham to Drinsey Nook. They stopped at the Sun Inn at Saxilby for a meal. For Mary, it was her last supper. On the road between Saxilby and Drinsey Nook, at the place where the road to Harby crosses the road to Doddington, Tom grabbed a wooden club and beat Mary's skull to pulp, nearly pounding it off her neck. Then he dumped her body in a ditch.

The body was discovered the next day by two workmen. Mary's corpse was taken back to the Sun Inn for an inquest, then buried in Saxilby.

Someone recalled seeing Tom walking around carrying a

wooden club on the day of the murder, so on November 6 he was arrested in Lincoln, at the Packhorse Inn. He stood trial on March 12, 1806. The trial lasted five hours, with twenty witnesses called. Their evidence was all circumstantial, but it was enough to convince the jury. They returned a guilty verdict in just a few minutes.

The judge, Justice Robert Graham, was repulsed by the beating death of an innocent, heavily pregnant woman. He sentenced Tom Otter to death by hanging. At first, the judge was going to let doctors dissect Tom's dead body, but then he changed his mind. He swapped that postmortem punishment for something much more gruesome.

Two days after his trial, Tom Otter was hanged at midday. Then his body was taken to the crossroads on March 20. (Again, a little more math. He was hanged on March 14. He was still above ground on March 20.) His body was shellacked with pitch to slow decomposition, then stuffed into an iron cage, hoisted thirty feet into the air, and hung from a post for people to gawk at.

There were ... technical difficulties in carrying out the gibbeting sentence. The iron cage was made a little too small for the 5' 9" Otter, so his tarred corpse was really crammed in there. The workmen who were putting the cage up on the pole struggled with the high, bitter March winds that were sweeping across the countryside that day, and it took the workmen three tries to get the grisly thing up to a height of thirty feet. On the second try, the cage and its grisly contents came crashing down—and landed on top of one of the workmen. He died of his injuries the next day.

The gibbet and its disgusting contents soon became a destination for Sunday picnickers and tourists. Young men would clamber up the post and try to grab a body part for a souvenir, as their giggling, squealing girlfriends egged them on from the ground. Gypsies would happily camp near the decomposing remains; they knew that the locals kept a wary distance from the gibbet after dark, and the wanderers could camp there safely and be left in peace.

The gibbet stood until 1850. (Last bit of math, I promise: that means Tom's corpse was swinging in the breeze for 45 years.) It was then that the cage was taken down, and what little was left of Tom Otter was buried beside the road. The post and cage were broken up, and the chunks sold as souvenirs.

But wait—we're done with the ghastly bits, now here comes the ghostly part. After the trial, the owner of the Sun Inn acquired the murder weapon. On the second anniversary of the murder, in 1807, the club was found under the gibbet, covered in what looked like fresh blood. The same thing happened the next year, and the year after that. Some folks thought the innkeeper was pulling a cheap publicity stunt to bring in more business for the inn in which poor doomed Mary Temporal, nee Kirkham, ate her last meal. But the innkeeper was just as baffled as everyone else. He sold the murder weapon to the owner of the Peeweet Inn at Drinsey Nook—and the next November 3, it turned up under the gibbet again. The owner nailed it to the wall with iron staples, but again, it showed up in its usual spot on November 3. The next year, a couple of guys were assigned to watch the cudgel to make sure it didn't go walkabout, but they fell asleep. And sure enough, it was found under the gibbet the next morning, glistening red. The Bishop of Lincoln confiscated the club and had it burned.

The story's not quite over yet, though. A few years later, a priest heard the deathbed confession of a workman named John Dunberly, who admitted that he had been a witness to Mary Kirkham's murder, but he had been reluctant to come forward. He told the priest that Tom had solicitously helped Mary to a seat at the edge of the road, then had taken the club and swung it at her head. Dunberly described the sound of the blow as being "like smashing a turnip."

His reticence cost him dearly. Every year on November 3, he would be woken from sleep by the ghost of Tom Otter. The ghost would lead him to wherever the murder weapon happened to be at the time. Then the ghost of Mary would join them, and Dunberly would be forced to accompany the two spirits to the crossroads where the moldering corpse of Tom Otter hung. Then the two spirits would reenact the horrific killing.

Dunberly spent all year, for several years, waiting in

agonized suspense for the ghosts' annual visit. When the bishop had the club destroyed, the grisly reenactment stopped. But Dunberly was so traumatized by his experience that it took him until he was on his deathbed to summon up the courage to tell his tale.

Quick Justice? (1810)

Ernest Augustus, the Duke of Cumberland and Queen Victoria's uncle, was one of the most feared men in England. He was, to begin with, fearsome to look at. He'd been terribly wounded by a blow to the head in battle in May 1794. He had gruesome scars on his face, and he'd lost an eye. He also had a reputation for being unscrupulous, overbearing, and sexually adventurous. He was generally considered the black sheep of an already weird family.

In the early morning hours of May 31, 1810, it seemed that fate had caught up to Cumberland. He was attacked with his own sword as he slept. Although the weapon was razor-sharp, the assailant used the flat of the blade, not the newly-sharpened edge. Even so, the first blow split Cumberland's skull wide open, cutting so deeply it exposed his brain. Three more blows fell as he stumbled from his bed. With a rush of adrenaline, Cumberland yelled, "Neale! Neale! I am murdered!"

Cornelius Neale, the duke's valet, came rushing in, but found Cumberland alone in his room. His attacker had fled, leaving the bloody sword on the floor. Neale made sure Cumberland was safe, and called for a doctor. Then he went in search of the would-be murderer.

The only member of the household unaccounted for was Cumberland's valet, Joseph Sellis. His slippers, though, were found in the duke's bedroom closet—the place where, it was thought, the attacker had hidden before slinking out to attack Cumberland. Sellis had to be found.

Two servants were sent to Sellis's room. As they approached, they heard a disgusting gurgling sound. They threw open the door and found Sellis lying on his bed, drowning in his own blood. His throat had been slashed with a straight razor so deeply that only his spine had stopped the blade.

An inquest was thrown together, and it was decided that Sellis had tried to murder Cumberland. Failing at that, he had retreated to his room and committed suicide. Court gossip, though, said otherwise. Sellis's head had been nearly severed from his body. There was no way, people muttered, that such a wound could be self-inflicted.

To add to the confusion, they pointed out that Sellis's hands were clean, but there was a basin filled with bloody water on his nightstand. So did Sellis almost cut his own head off, then stop to wash his hands? That didn't make any sense either.

The straight razor found at the scene was nowhere near Sellis's hand. But a policeman had an explanation for that. Sergeant Joseph Creighton admitted that he'd picked it up to look at it, then had set it down several feet away. The crime scene hadn't just been contaminated; it had been rearranged.

If Sellis hadn't committed suicide, who had killed him? The alternative scenarios were varied and imaginative. Sellis had found Cumberland in bed with his wife. Or Cumberland had seduced Sellis's daughter, who had killed herself when she discovered she was pregnant. Or Sellis and Cumberland had been lovers, and when the other valet, Neale, had been hired, Neale had taken Sellis's place in the duke's bed. Or, or, or … the mystery has never been solved.

Maybe that's why Joseph Sellis haunts St. James Palace. His shadowy figure still roams the halls, accompanied by the coppery stink of fresh blood. Palace staff often report feeling as if they're being watched, and small objects get moved or go missing. The haunting is particularly severe in the room where Sellis was killed. A few unfortunate witnesses claim to have seen the specter of Joseph Sellis sitting in his bed, propped up on the edge of death, his mouth hanging open over a grisly wound in his neck, his head nearly severed from his body.

Murder in the Red Barn (1827)

It's an old story. Poor girl catches the eye of son of well-to-do family, the two fall in love and make plans to elope, guy gets cold feet and dumps the girl. But in the case of William Corder and Maria Marten, there are a few interesting wrinkles.

Murder, for a start.

Maria Marten was 24 when she started seeing 22-year-old William Corder, a son of the local squire. Maria was a pretty girl who had no trouble picking up men—she'd already had two children, one of them by William's older brother Thomas. That child died in infancy, but another son survived. Thomas wanted nothing to do with Maria after the kid came along, but he did send Maria money for the boy's support.

William was no prize. His nickname at school was "Foxey", for his sly, furtive manner. He was known as a womanizer and a serial committer of fraud. He sold his father's pigs illegally, helped a local thief steal another pig, and forged a check for 93 pounds. After the fraudulent pig-selling incident, William was sent off to London, but was called back home when his brother Thomas (Maria's baby daddy) drowned trying to cross a frozen pond. As it turned out, all three of William's brothers, and his father, all died within a year and a half of each other, leaving William and his mother to run their farm.

William wanted to keep his relationship with Maria secret, but that proved difficult—she gave birth to their child in 1827. (This child also died, and may have been murdered.) Even with all William's flaws, she was keen to marry him.

William was not so enamored of the idea. To keep Maria quiet, on May 18 he suggested (in front of Maria's stepmother,

Ann Marten) that he and Maria should elope. He hinted that Maria was in danger of being arrested and prosecuted for having bastard children. He told Maria to get dressed in men's clothes, so she could make her way to the meeting place unnoticed, and asked her to meet him at the Red Barn.

After that, both Maria and William disappeared.

William turned up a bit later, claiming that Maria was … somewhere close. When her family asked where, William hemmed and hawed, saying he couldn't yet bring Maria home as his wife without getting in trouble with his relatives. He had excuse after excuse as to why Maria was incommunicado: she wasn't feeling well. Or she'd hurt her hand and couldn't write a letter to her family. Or she did write, and the letter somehow got lost in the mail. Under pressure to produce his wife, William soon left the area. He sent several letters back to Maria's family, saying they were married and living on the Isle of Wight, but somehow, no one bought it.

Maria's stepmother was one of the most suspicious. She began telling people she'd had dreams that Maria had been murdered and buried in the Red Barn. On April 19, 1828, almost a year after William and Maria had eloped, she convinced her husband to investigate. He dug around in one of the grain storage bins and discovered Maria's badly decomposed remains in a sack. William's green handkerchief was around her neck.

Maria's body was taken to the Cock Inn in Polstead for an inquest. Her sister Ann identified the body—Maria's hair and clothing were still recognizable. Also, Maria was missing a tooth, and the same tooth was missing from the jawbone of the corpse. The inquest couldn't establish the exact cause of Maria's death; she could have been strangled, because William's handkerchief was around her neck. Other wounds suggested she'd been shot, and William had been seen with a loaded pistol that day, right before Maria's disappearance. There was also evidence that Maria had been stabbed in the eye, maybe with William's short sword, but the damage to her eye socket could have been caused by her father's spade when he was digging her up.

Whatever killed her, Maria Marten was undeniably dead.

Mr. Ayres, the constable in Polstead, and James Lea, an officer in the London police force, quickly tracked William to Everly Grove House, a boarding house for ladies in Brentford. And what was William doing in a ladies' boarding house? He was running it, with his new wife, Mary Moore. He'd met Moore by placing a "lonely hearts" ad in the newspaper. Out of over a hundred replies, he chose her. He was brought back to Polstead and, because of the wounds on Maria's corpse, was charged with murder.

The indictment charged William with "murdering Maria Marten, by feloniously and wilfully shooting her with a pistol through the body, and likewise stabbing her with a dagger." Wanting to cover all the bases, and to avoid any chance of a mistrial, the court indicted William Corder on nine charges, including forgery (and, of course, murder).

The prosecution argued that Maria knew about William's shady dealings, and that made her a threat to him. Also, William had stolen money that his brother Thomas had sent to Maria for his son's upkeep. Ann Marten testified about the dreams she'd said she'd been having. (Although Ann may have made these up out of whole cloth. Remember how I said that she'd "dreamed" that Maria had been murdered and buried? Turns out that she started having these dreams a few days after William married Mary Moore. To add even more intrigue to this story, Ann was only a few years older than Maria, and she may have been stepping out with William herself. Ann and William may have planned Maria's murder to get Maria out of the way so they could continue their affair. Ann's jealousy over Moore could have led her to rat William out for the murder.)

There was more. Thomas Marten described digging up his daughter's body. And George Marten, Maria's ten-year-old brother, said he'd seen William with a loaded pistol before the murder, and had later seen him walking away from the barn carrying a pickaxe.

In his own defense, William said that he and Maria had argued in the barn, but he'd walked away. As he was leaving, he'd heard a pistol shot ring out. He'd run back to the barn and found Maria dead, with one of William's pistols beside her.

Nobody believed this story, mostly because it wasn't true. It took the jury just 35 minutes to find William guilty. He was hanged on August 11, 1828. Before the execution, William confessed to what really happened. Encouraged by his wife and the prison chaplain, he said he hadn't stabbed Maria, but he had accidentally shot her in the eye as they argued.

Corder's body was taken from the gallows and, as was common practice at the time, given to the anatomists for dissection. His skin was tanned and used to cover a book containing an account of the trial. Part of Corder's scalp, with the ear still attached, was put on display in a shop window. His skeleton was disassembled, boiled clean, then put back together to go on display at the West Suffolk Hospital. (Apparently, someone gifted with business acumen—and a morbid sense of humor—rigged it so that when a gawker approached the display case, a mechanism was tripped, and lifted Corder's bony arm to point to the donation box.)

But it was Corder's skull that had the most adventures after his death. For some reason, the Murder in the Red Barn captured ridiculous amounts of public attention. Over five thousand people traipsed past to see Corder's body after the execution. People were scrambling for souvenirs, including lengths of the rope used to hang Corder, and locks of Maria's hair. Even the barn was stripped for parts. Planks were removed from the walls, broken up, and turned into toothpicks. One Dr. Kilner decided to get himself a primo souvenir—he stole Corder's skull and put a spare skull from the anatomy lab in its place. Dr. Kilner had Corder's skull polished, and he enshrined it in a fancy box which he kept in his drawing room.

Any ghost story enthusiast could have told Kilner that this was a mistake. People who came into the drawing room felt a sense of unease … then the noises started. Doors slammed violently. Hammering and sobbing sounds were heard coming from the box that held the skull. The servants said that a man in old-fashioned clothes was hanging around the house, but always disappeared before anyone got a good look at him. They said he was waiting to see the doctor, but would vanish by the time the doctor arrived for his appointment.

Kilner refused to admit that there was some really strange stuff happening in his house. But one night, he was woken up by a loud noise. He ran into the hall, and saw the drawing room door being opened by a white hand—just a hand. An explosion rocked the room, nearly blowing the door off its hinges, and a blast of icy-cold air engulfed the doctor, blowing out his candle. He scrabbled for a match, managed to light it—and saw the skull sitting undamaged on the floor, grinning at him, surrounded by the fragments of the box in which it had been kept.

Kilner knew he had to get rid of the skull, but how? If he brought it back to the anatomy lab, someone would surely notice its glossy polish atop the dull rest of the skeleton. His theft would be discovered, and he would be disgraced. He couldn't just throw the skull away—who knew what supernatural hijinks would happen then? He decided to give the skull to F.C. Hopkins, a retired prison official, who had bought the jail where Corder had been hanged. Surely he'd appreciate the collectors value of Corder's skull. He told Hopkins, "You already own Corder's cell, and the gallows where they hanged him; perhaps it won't harm you to look after his skull."

Hopkins accepted the grisly memento, but he discovered it wasn't going to be a walk in the park for him either. He picked the skull up at Kilner's house, wrapped it in a silk handkerchief, and started home. On the way, he tripped and sprained his ankle. He dropped the skull, which rolled down the road past a lady who was out for a walk. She fainted.

Dr. Kilner and Mr. Hopkins both suffered a run of bad luck, and in a few months, they had both gone bankrupt. Hopkins finally gave up and bribed a gravedigger in a secluded graveyard to bury the skull in consecrated ground. That decision turned out to benefit Kilner, too. Both men's bad luck eased up after that.

The Sayre Murders (1833)

The Sayre home, built in 1749 by John Sayre, was a peaceful place, a place where generations of the Sayre family lived happily, the place where Alexander Hamilton proposed to his beloved Eliza. But in 1833, someone arrived at the Sayre house who would throw everything into turmoil, and leave the Sayre home with the reputation of being one of the most haunted places in New Jersey.

Antoine LeBlanc was a French immigrant who came to the United States from Germany. He came to seek his fortune, as he had big plans for his share of the New World's wealth. LeBlanc was from a good family, and he had plans to marry an equally well-heeled young German woman, Marie Smicht. He'd been in the country only three days when he was hired by Samuel Sayre to work the family farm.

At first, LeBlanc was thrilled. He had a job, even if it was just chopping wood and slopping hogs. Not bad for a guy who could barely speak English. But even with his limited communication skills, LeBlanc soon realized he had gotten a really bum deal. In exchange for his menial labor, he was to receive lodging in a small room in the dank basement of the Sayre house ... and that was it. No wages, no cash, nothing.

LeBlanc was peeved. How could he afford to save his money to get back to Germany and marry his ladylove if he wasn't even getting paid for the work he did? And it was crap work, too. Even worse, since he was the low man on the household totem pole, he had to take orders from everyone—Samuel, his wife Sarah, even their servant Phoebe. That really rankled. Soon, LeBlanc had worked himself into a righteous fury. If he couldn't earn a decent wage, he'd steal it.

On May 11, about two weeks after he'd been hired, LeBlanc took his revenge. He went out to a tavern and got all liquored up. He came back to the farm around 10:30 pm, and called Samuel Sayre out to the stable, saying there was a problem with the horses. Samuel, suspecting nothing, came out to the barn at LeBlanc's call, carrying a candle. LeBlanc met him with a shovel to the face, splattering Samuel's brains all over his coat.

Next, LeBlanc killed Sarah Sayre, again braining her with the shovel, and finishing her off with a kick in the head. He hid the bodies under a pile of manure in the barn. Then he went to tie up the loose end. Phoebe was asleep in her bedroom on the second floor when LeBlanc caved in her skull with one violent blow from a club.

After his killing spree, LeBlanc took whatever portable valuables he could find, stuffing them into pillowcases. He stole a horse from the barn and headed off into the darkness. What he didn't realize was that one of the pillowcases was leaking swag. LeBlanc left a trail of stolen goods behind him as he fled. Some of the items had Samuel Sayre's monogram on them. The next morning, a friend of the Sayres, Lewis Halsey, found the dropped items. Fearing the Sayres had been robbed, he rounded up some neighbors and they went to the Sayre farm to investigate. What they found was a whole lot worse than a simple robbery.

The barn was drenched in blood spatter. The search party found the murdered couple underneath the manure pile in the barn, and Phoebe dead in her bed. Sheriff George Ludlow set off to look for the killer. The sheriff had little trouble finding the killer, because LeBlanc hadn't gotten far. (Also, he left a trail of breadcrumbs—or rather, small valuables monogrammed with Samuel Sayre's initials—behind him as he went.) He'd planned to go to New York to find a ship bound for Germany. He got as far as the Mosquito Tavern in Hackensack Meadows when he got thirsty and stopped in for a mug of beer. LeBlanc was sitting with his beer, with Sayre's pillowcase next to him, when he saw Ludlow coming to the tavern. LeBlanc bolted for the back door when Ludlow came in, but he was collared immediately.

The trial of Antoine LeBlanc for the murders began—and ended—on August 13. The jury took just twenty minutes to find him guilty, and there was no appeal. LeBlanc was sentenced to hang.

In the afternoon of September 6, LeBlanc was led to the gallows. He was to be hanged by a modern design, which jerked the condemned man upward, rather than dropping the floor out from underneath him. Judge Stephen Vail also happened to own an iron works, so he took it upon himself to provide the special gallows, designed with a pulley system to hoist LeBlanc eight feet up, so everyone could get a good look at him. A crowd of somewhere between 10,000 and 12,000 pushing, jeering spectators showed up with picnic lunches to Morristown for the spectacle. It was quite the crowd, as the town only had a population of 2,500 at the time.

The counterweight dropped, and LeBlanc was jerked eight feet into the air. He twitched for two minutes or so, then was still. His body was left to hang for 35 minutes.

If his death was relatively peaceful, what happened next was decidedly less so. Judge Gabriel Ford had decreed that after the execution, LeBlanc's body was to be given to Dr. Isaac Canfield for dissection. (This was actually standard procedure for those times, and we'll see it quite a bit in this book. The custom served a couple of purposes: it was a good way for doctors to study the human body. Cadavers were in short supply in those days, and it was better than robbing graves to get their dissection subjects. Also, it was a final indignity for the condemned.)

Canfield and another doctor, Dr. Joseph Henry, had a grand old time with LeBlanc's corpse. They decided to use the fresh body for some experiments in galvanism, which is basically running electrical currents through muscles to make them jump. They made incisions in LeBlanc's arms and legs, exposing the nerves, and attached electrodes to them. They got his limbs to twitch, his eyes to roll, and even managed to draw his lips back in a slight smile.

But the indignities visited on LeBlanc's corpse didn't stop there, oh no. After the doctors got done using LeBlanc as their own personal life-size game of Operation, they sent him to the Atno Tannery in Morristown, where he was skinned and his hide was turned into purses, wallets, lampshades, and even book jackets. They became treasured souvenirs in the Morristown area, being handed down as family heirlooms. (The local newspaper *The Jerseyman* called them "charming little keepsakes.") Sheriff Ludlow himself signed the souvenirs, attesting to their authenticity.

The whole gruesome incident, the murders, the hanging, the epidermal arts-and-crafts, paved the way for a really resplendent haunting. Since 1833, the Sayre house has been crazy haunted. The house was eventually turned into a restaurant, which had many incarnations. In 1946, the house became the Wincerter Turnpike Inn. In 1957, a mysterious fire ripped through the building. In 1960, it was renovated and became the Wedgewood Inn. Over the years it has had many owners and many names: South Street, Argyle's Restaurant, Society Hill, Phoebe's Restaurant (yes, named after the innocent servant), and most recently, Jimmy's Haunt.

And through all the changes, the ghosts have been there. Phoebe's bedroom, on the second floor, became the banquet room of the establishment. A mirror hung on the wall, and Phoebe would often appear in it, staring dully, blonde hair hanging limply around her pale face. Startled waitresses would regularly drop trays of glassware when the phantom appeared in the mirror. Phoebe's room was always noticeably colder than the other parts of the building, and many people remarked on the eerie presence they felt in the room.

Doors opened and closed by themselves, and employees were spooked by the sound of footsteps on the second floor when no one was up there. One waitress working in Phoebe's room saw a bloody hand reach out from one of the paintings on the wall. Other employees refused to go down into the basement alone after a bartender saw a lit candle moving around with no one holding it.

In 1991, the restaurant changed ownership yet again and was named Society Hill. On the night of the grand opening, the new owners got a paranormal welcome: as a punch bowl was being filled for the party, it inexplicably cracked in half, sending punch flooding all over the counter.

Sadly, the Sayre House no longer stands. Jimmy's Haunt was demolished in 2007 to make way for a Commerce Bank. Where the resident ghosts ended up is anyone's guess.

Jack Osteen's Poetic Justice (1834)

The Merchants' Exchange Building in Philadelphia is home to a very strange haunting. This is a tale of love, devotion ... and revenge.

Harold Thorn was a wealthy businessman who lived in Philadelphia in the 1830s. He'd gotten filthy rich because he was a conniving, unscrupulous, greedy, ill-tempered bastard. Nobody liked him, but his business contacts were extensive, and he was at the Merchants' Exchange Building quite often, so his colleagues had to put up with him.

Another fellow who was often at the building—albeit outside—was Jack Osteen, a blind beggar. He hung around outside the halls of commerce, where the businessmen tethered their horses, hoping someone would hire him for any of the few jobs of which he was capable. Despite his handicap, Jack was friendly, always quick with a song or a funny story as he waited for odd jobs. Jack was kind to all, and he especially loved horses. He petted the businessmen's mounts, stroking their velvety noses, and whenever he had a few extra pennies, he bought apples to treat his equine friends.

One of the horses that bonded with Jack belonged to Harold Thorn. The horse adored Jack, and would toss his head and refuse to be tied to the hitching post unless he was put as close to Jack as he could get. (Knowing Thorn's temperament, it's likely that the moments he spent with Jack were the only time the horse knew kindness.)

On November 12, 1834, Thorn was in a foul mood. He had lost quite a lot of money at the Exchange that day, and by the time he stomped outside, he had worked himself into a towering rage.

As Thorn stalked over to his horse, he bumped into Jack. Jack, blind, tried to scramble out of Thorn's way, but ended up stepping on Thorn's expensive shoes. Thorn snapped, his barely-controlled fury breaking loose. He beat Jack with his walking stick—the silver head of the cane flashed as the blows rained down on the beggar, and soon, the silver was slicked scarlet with blood. By the time someone caught Thorn's arm and stopped him, he had beaten Jack Osteen to death.

The crowd of men was stunned into silence. No one dared to move. Suddenly, Thorn's horse screamed in rage. He reared up and brought his ironshod hooves crashing down on his master. Thorn was gravely wounded, and later died from the attack.

Ever since then, Thorn has spent his afterlife in terror. His ghost appears after sundown at the Merchants' Exchange Building, standing at the place where he met his well-deserved end. He stands there for a moment—then the sound of approaching hoofbeats on cobblestone rings in the air. The ghost looks around, fear sharpening his features ... then he vanishes.

Haunted By A Dream (1847)

In the 1840s, a fellow by the name of Foxworthy resided in Louisville, Kentucky. He lived in a boardinghouse on Walnut Street. A hard worker, he was also frugal, and saved the money he earned. But like many folks in the mid-nineteenth century, he was wary of trusting a bank with that hard-earned scratch. Instead, he preferred to keep it close, hidden away in a trunk in his room.

This would have been a fairly sound plan, except that at some point, Foxworthy must have bragged about his stash of cash. One of the other residents of the boardinghouse, a blacksmith named Whittinghill, heard about the simoleons socked away in Foxworthy's room. Whittinghill had ambitions of his own—he was head over heels in love with a young lady. But his blacksmithing was not making him as rich as he wanted her to think he was. So, Whittinghill thought, why not take his finances into his own hands? He knew that Foxworthy had $100 squirrelled away.

And he wanted it for himself.

On the morning of July 3, 1847, Whittinghill invited Foxworthy to go hunting with him. The two men rowed a small boat across the Ohio River into the forests of southern Indiana, just outside Jeffersonville, in search of game. Foxworthy carried a gun, and Whittinghill was armed with a club fashioned of rock-solid hickory wood. Both men went into the woods … but only Whittinghill came out. He got the jump on the unsuspecting Foxworthy, bashed his brains out, and hid both corpse and murder weapon in the thick woods.

Whittinghill was not the sharpest tool in the shed. He had

a plan that was about as blunt-force as the hickory club. He went back to the boardinghouse and oh-so-casually had a chat with the landlord. Whittinghill showed the landlord a note supposedly signed by Foxworthy, suggesting that Foxworthy wanted his trunk to be given to his dear friend Whittinghill. When asked where Foxworthy had gone, Whittinghill muttered something about Foxworthy finding work in Jeffersonville.

This flimsy explanation, and Whittinghill's request to take possession of Foxworthy's trunk, went over about as well as you'd expect. In addition, plenty of people had seen the two men leave the boardinghouse, and had also seen Whittinghill come back without his club. The landlord didn't believe a word of Whittinghill's story, and refused to hand over the trunk. His plan foiled, Whittinghill slunk away.

The next morning, Joseph Nagle of Jeffersonville was wandering in the woods looking for material to build boats with. While searching, he tripped over a mound of dirt and leaves—quite literally. It was the shallow grave of Foxworthy. Obviously, though, at the time Nagle had no idea whose corpse he'd just stumbled over. He went to the authorities, who didn't know the corpse's identity either.

So, they crowdsourced it. The body was put on display at a local market, where as many people could see it as possible. The plan worked; hundreds of people saw the body, including the landlord of the boardinghouse in Louisville. He identified the corpse as Foxworthy, and told the authorities that he strongly suspected that Whittinghill was the murderer. The police agreed with this theory, and picked Whittinghill up in Jeffersonville.

But the authorities had a problem. Foxworthy had obviously been bludgeoned to death. And loads of people had seen Whittinghill leaving Louisville with a club, and returning without it—and without Foxworthy. Every bit of the circumstantial evidence pointed to Whittinghill being the murderer. But without a murder weapon, authorities were unlikely to get a conviction. Volunteers searched the woods, but came up empty-handed.

That is, until one of the searchers, Thomas Morgan, had a strange dream. He dreamed he was walking in those very woods. You've had dreams like that, right? Where you've done something for so long during the day, that you keep doing it in your sleep? But now, the ghost of Foxworthy was tagging along with Morgan. Man and spirit wandered the trails that Morgan had spent hours of his waking life searching. Foxworthy's ghost led the dreaming Morgan to a swamp, and showed him the hickory club hidden under a rotting log.

Morgan jerked awake and bounded out of bed, newly energized. He hurried back out to the woods and wandered until he realized that the landscape looked oddly familiar—and not because he'd seen it in his previous searching. This was the very swamp that Foxworthy had shown him in his dream.

Amazed, Morgan looked around and spotted the fallen, rotted log that Foxworthy's ghost had pointed out to him. Morgan picked up a stout stick and started poking around in the mucky soil under the log. A few prods brought up the murder weapon, still slimed with blood, hair, and brain matter.

Whittinghill was sentenced to death. Before his sentence was carried out, though, he died in jail. It was commonly said that he died from remorse.

A Marriage Gone Sour (1850)

John McCaffary left Ireland and came to America in May 1837. He liked America so much, he applied for citizenship in 1846. In August 1847, he reached another milestone: he bought a plot of land in Kenosha, Wisconsin (then known as Southport), from Charles and Caroline Durkee. Not long after, he built a two-story brick house on the lot. And on May 2, 1848, he married Bridget McKean at St. James Church in Southport.

Two years into their marriage ... something happened. Around midnight on July 22, 1850, neighbors awoke to a woman's screams. The cries of "Oh, John, spare me!" were heard over a block away. Neighbors rushed to the McCaffary house, and found John coming out of the backyard. Some people said they heard faint splashing sounds coming from an abandoned well in the backyard, but those sounds soon stopped.

The neighbors, concerned, asked John if Bridget was in the well. He replied vaguely that *someone* was in the well. The neighbors rushed over, but it was too late. A look into the murky water revealed a body dressed in a white shirt ... a bruised body that was indeed Bridget McCaffary.

Bystanders also found John's hat and one shoe in the well. The other shoe was between the well and the house, and was slicked with muck from the stagnant well. There was only about 18 to 20 inches of water in the well. Investigators put the picture together pretty quickly: John McCaffary had tried to drown his wife in the well. When that didn't work, he stomped on her head until she died.

John was tried for murder in July 1851. He was found guilty and sentenced to death by hanging. He didn't testify in his own defense. And he never gave a reason for his heinous attack on his wife.

According to local stories, somewhere between two and three thousand people witnessed the hanging. But the hanging wasn't the traditional "drop the guy through the trapdoor" affair. It was much less humane than that—the victim was raised into the air, meaning that instead of (hopefully) a nice clean snap of the neck, the condemned slowly strangled to death. After McCaffary had hung suspended for eight minutes, doctors checked his pulse. It had only slowed slightly, not stopped, so they let him hang ten minutes more. The execution of John McCaffary was the first and last capital punishment carried out in Wisconsin. (Because of this dubious honor, the McCaffary House was listed on the National Register of Historic Places in 1978. And John McCaffary was buried quietly and without ceremony. His grave was unmarked until 2001, when the Wisconsin Historical Society erected a marker at his burial site.) The hanging was so gruesomely botched that the citizens of Wisconsin were outraged. The death penalty was repealed in the state in 1853, and has never yet been reinstated.

Bridget McCaffary did not rest easily, even though her husband paid for his crime. John told a newspaper reporter that Bridget had visited him on several occasions during the days leading up to his execution, to taunt him with his impending doom.

For the next half a century, the murder of Bridget McCaffary stained the house and the well where she met her end. Articles appeared in the paper every so often, claiming that tenants who rented the house moved out in pretty short order. Disturbing noises, they said, kept them awake all night, and it was near impossible to get a good night's sleep.

The McCaffary house, and the house next door to it, are still haunted by the unfortunate Bridget. (The house next door didn't escape the violence; John chased Bridget around the yards of both houses before grabbing her and throwing her headfirst into the well on the McCaffary property.) One owner told the *Kenosha News* in 1999 that he had been sitting in the neighboring house with a friend when the friend saw the startling sight of a woman's face in the window—a window that was ten feet off the ground.

Later, in the McCaffary house, the former owner was sitting with friends when one person saw an apparition in the living room doorway. Another time, the owner clearly heard footsteps in the upstairs rooms when he was alone in the house except for his dog. The house had been divided for a while into upper and lower apartments, and none of the tenants stayed very long, explaining that disturbing noises kept them awake all night. The paranormal activity doesn't seem to be threatening in nature; people just say the house has a "bad feel" to it. When these residents leave the house to move elsewhere, they report feeling much lighter in spirit, as if some supernatural oppression has lifted.

The McCaffary house has recently been restored to its original function as a single-family residence. The new owners haven't reported any activity … yet.

Insanity (1855)

The McLean County Historical Society, in Bloomington, Illinois, was founded in 1892. At first, the aim was simply to do presentations on local history. These papers, and transcribed talks, were the genesis of its collection. But soon, people in the community started donating ... things. The outfit turned into the McLean County Museum of History, which opened in 1903. For decades, collection acquisition continued, and the museum was soon stuffed into its digs, without the room to properly display its growing collection.

In 1992, the museum moved into its present home, the Old McLean County Courthouse, built soon after 1900. (This was the fourth courthouse built on the square; the first two were built in 1832 and 1836. The third, built in 1868 of limestone and other fireproof materials—at least on the outside—burned from the inside out in the citywide fire of 1900.) In 1996, the museum won an Award of Excellence from the Association of Museums for its Evergreen Cemetery Discovery Walk. The museum has also been home to the Cruisin' With Lincoln on 66 Visitors Center since April 2015.

The museum is a grand building that looks every inch a courthouse of importance. The visitors center was built in 2014, and before construction began, the museum did an archaeological excavation on the south side of the building. This was the site of the second courthouse, the one in which Abraham Lincoln practiced law. A brass bar set into the pavement now marks the southern wall of that vanished building.

The McLean County Museum of History keeps the history of Bloomington alive ... and not just with award-winning exhibits and tours. The museum hums with activity—and with residual hauntings. Witnesses can sometimes experience burning sensations and sharp chest pains. No one was killed in the 1900 blaze, but a resident running away from the fall of burning cinders suffered a massive heart attack and died.

There is also the curious experience of feeling an "angry" sensation along one's arm, especially when visiting the courtrooms of the building, some of which are preserved as exhibits. To understand this peculiar residual haunting, we have to look again to history.

Most of Abraham Lincoln's cases in Bloomington and other towns in the area were property disputes or other minor squabbles. Lincoln's friend Ward Hill Lamon, however, had been elected state's attorney, and he got the rare murder cases. One of Lamon's first murder cases turned out to be a doozy. At first, it seemed pretty cut and dried, but the further the case progressed, the murkier and more complicated it became. Lamon asked Lincoln for his help with the prosecution.

Here's what happened: two men, Anson Rusk and Isaac Wyant, didn't get along for whatever reason. In June 1855, Wyant attacked Rusk with a large knife. Rusk, trying to avoid getting cut, drew a pistol and shot Wyant in the arm. The wound was so bad, the arm had to be amputated, and Wyant swore he'd get his revenge.

In October 1855, Wyant started telling people around town that he was going to take a trip to Indiana. He never left town. Instead, he lay in wait for Rusk. Wyant hung around the town of Clinton for several days, waiting for his chance to attack Rusk. On Friday October 12, Rusk came to town, and Wyant started tailing his sworn enemy. He caught up with Rusk at the courthouse. Rusk went into the office of the county clerk and was standing behind the stove with his arms folded. Wyant burst through the door, aimed a revolver at Rusk, and started firing. The first ball hit Rusk in the side, the second in the shoulder, and the third hit his arm. Rusk fell to the floor writhing in agony, but Wyant wasn't finished. A local newspaper reported with ghoulish thoroughness: "Wyant then stood over the fallen man, put the pistol to his head and fired the fourth shot, the ball passing entirely through the head, and from the orifice it made oozed the brains."

Rusk died almost an hour later, never having regained consciousness. Wyant ran from the scene, but was collared only a short distance away from the courthouse. He was clapped into prison and put in chains. The horrified witness who happened to be in the clerk's office at the time of the murder was willing to testify.

Even worse for Wyant, Rusk's wife was pregnant at the time. The violent death of her husband sent her into labor, and she gave birth prematurely. At the time of the newspaper article, written a week later on October 19 ("Murder", *DeWitt Courier*, October 19, 1855, People v. Wyant), neither mother nor child was expected to live. The article pointed out, "If they die Wyant will be a triple murderer, and consequently, he should suffer the severest penalty of the law."

In order to make sure Wyant got a fair trial, there was a change of venue. The trial was moved to the McLean County Courthouse, about 25 miles away from Clinton. The defense attorney was a lawyer named Leonard Swett, who was a good friend of Lincoln's. Swett was an excellent criminal defense attorney, and Lamon and Lincoln knew they were in for a fight.

Even with the responsible witness testifying that they'd seen Wyant come into the clerk's office and kill Rusk right in front of them, the defense had a reasonable argument. When Wyant's arm was amputated, the doctors doing the surgery used chloroform as an anesthetic. At the time, it was believed that a possible side effect of chloroform use was insanity.

Swett's witnesses testified that Wyant's bizarre, paranoid behavior only started after the loss of his arm. Since chloroform was used as the anesthetic, Swett argued convincingly that Wyant had become insane as a result. Lamon and Lincoln ended up losing the case. Wyant was found to be temporarily insane. He was acquitted of the murders, and committed to an insane asylum.

The case of The People v. Wyant was one of the earliest cases in American legal history in which an insanity defense resulted in acquittal for the accused. Soon after this trial, Lincoln was asked to take the case of a young man whose only hope was a plea of not guilty by reason of insanity. He bowed out of the request, and suggested his client ask Leonard Swett to defend him.

America's First Bank Robber (1863)

E dward Green was in trouble.

Green was the postmaster for the town of Malden, Massachusetts, near Boston. The job was a politically appointed position, and the pay wasn't great. In fact, it was a pittance. And Edward Green was hurting for money. His debts were threatening to overwhelm him.

On December 15, 1863, Green trudged through the snow to Malden Bank to make his pitiful deposit. As he conducted his business, he noticed something interesting. Frank Converse, the 17-year-old assistant cashier, was working alone.

That got Green to thinking. Banks had simply loads of money just sitting around. A bank would be a great place to get money—enough to get himself out of debt for good.

But Malden wasn't a big city. Everyone knew who the postmaster was. Green was also the town accountant, in charge of not only the postal money, but also the finances of the schools. If he decided to rob the bank—something no one had ever done before—he couldn't leave any witnesses.

That's why, when Edward Green returned to the bank, he was carrying his recently purchased Smith & Wesson pistol.

The young clerk was still alone. Green, as a well-respected town official, knew Frank. But that didn't stop him in the pursuit of his goal. He shot Frank Eugene Converse in the head. The kid dropped to the floor, and Green shot him again. Then he stole $5,000 and ran, leaving the teenager's body on the marble floor in a spreading pool of blood.

The murder made national headlines; after all, it was a first. No one in American history had ever had the audacity to rob a bank. This "first" came with the added tragedy of a murdered teenager.

The outpouring of grief for Frank Converse was immense. The Converse family was in the top tier of Malden society, and Frank was a popular kid. The Converses were members of the Baptist church in town—Elisha Converse, Frank's father, was a deacon there—but the church was undergoing renovations at the time. So Frank's funeral was held on December 18 at the Orthodox church. Over six hundred people attended the funeral, the cream of the town's business class. The Hayward Guard (a social group of young men, of which Frank had been a member) formed an honor guard for the body. All business in town was suspended during the funeral.

Two months passed, as the town and the Converse family grieved. Then, people in town began to notice something odd. The previously penniless Postmaster Green was suddenly paying off all his debts. All well and good ... but where had the money come from? Questions began to be asked. At first, no one suspected Green of the bank robbery and murder. After all, he was the town's postmaster. He held a position of trust.

But Green couldn't evade justice, and his guilt weighed heavily on him. He confessed to authorities in February 1864, just two months after committing the crimes. Investigators found some money hidden in a boot at Green's house. Green was also a volunteer fireman, and the rest of the stolen money turned up socked away in the attic of the firehouse. Edward Green was sentenced to death, and went to the gallows in April 1866.

Elisha Converse, Frank's father, was fantastically, massively wealthy—rich enough to provide a fitting memorial for his lost son. Elisha Slade Converse was a founder and president of the Malden Bank, the bank in which his son was murdered. He also founded the Boston Rubber Shoe Company. (Fun fact: Elisha was rich enough to own—and sell—a factory. The town of Haywardvill, Massachusetts, was established in 1858 when Nathaniel Hayward bought a shoe factory near Spot Pond Brook in Stoneham from Elisha Converse. That single factory soon grew into an industrial village, and Hayward and Charles

Goodyear later invented vulcanized rubber there.)

The income from Elisha's shoe empire made him wealthy enough to give back to his community, which he did freely and with an open hand. Converse gave money to build Malden Hospital and the School of Nursing, Malden City Hall—he was elected the first mayor of Malden in 1892 by thunderous acclaim—Malden Historical Society, the Malden Home for Aged Persons and Day Nursery, Malden YMCA, Malden Public Library, and Malden Auditorium, one of the finest theaters in the Boston area at the time. He also donated over 100 acres of land for the public Pine Banks Park.

It is the Malden Public Library that provides us with the connection to our ghost story. Elisha Converse and his wife, Mary, built the Converse Memorial Building in 1885 as a tribute to their oldest son Frank. The building was home to the Malden Public Library from 1885 to 1996, when the library moved to more modern digs next door. The Converses were great patrons of the arts, and the Converse Memorial Building was also an art gallery. Elisha died in 1904, and in his will, left $50,000 specifically to purchase art. This sum was added to the $15,000 that Mary Converse had willed the previous year. However, the first purchase on record was made in 1892, which suggests that the collection was started with funds earmarked when both Elisha and Mary were still alive.

Eventually, the Converse Memorial Building became home to forty-eight works of fine art. Several of the paintings in the collection date back to the building's dedication in 1885. The pride of these early works is a full-length portrait of Frank Converse, forever captured at 17 years old. On either side of Frank's portrait are paintings of Elisha and Mary. (A fellow named John Gardner also gets a shout-out via oil paint—in 1878, he donated $15,000 to purchase books, which formed the beginning of the library's collection when it opened in 1885.)

The Malden Public Library is located at 36 Salem Street, just a short distance from where Frank Converse's life was cruelly cut short. (The bank where Frank worked is now Faces Brewery.) It seems that the young man has chosen to spend his afterlife in the stunningly gorgeous library building.

The Converse Memorial Building, a Gilded Age showplace with high vaulted ceilings and rich burnished woodwork, is considered to be one of architect H. H. Richardson's finest works, and was made a National Historic Landmark in 1987. It's also home to Frank's spirit. The young man occasionally moves furniture, and sometimes reaches out to patrons—literally.

An anonymous witness spoke of being in the basement of the library when they felt a hand on the back of their neck. As soon as they moved, the sensation went away. But ten seconds later, the phantom touch was back. "It was the most terrifying thing I've ever experienced," the witness reported.

Sam Baltrusis, noted paranormal author, swears he saw a chair move in the Converse Memorial Building, "as if an invisible force were taking a seat at the old-school library." The library has also made an appearance on a *Dead Files* episode (on the Travel Channel) called "Dark Inheritance."

The Malden Public Library enthusiastically embraces its resident ghost. And the town of Malden has not forgotten its lost son, either. Michael Cloherty has written a fictional treatment of the killing, entitled *Abel Bodied: Murder at the Malden Bank*. Cloherty recently gave a reading from the book at Hugh O'Neill's, a pub that was once the office of Postmaster Edward Green. The evening's festivities included a benefit drawing of a signed and numbered hardcover copy of the book. True to the Converses' legacy of public giving, the proceeds from the drawing, and from the sales of the next sixteen copies of the book, were donated to Bread of Life. This local charity distributes food to homeless people and other isolated folks. Why donate the proceeds from the first seventeen sales, you might ask? Simple—in honor of the seventeen years of Frank Converse's life. I think that's just beautiful.

The Ghost That Wasn't (1871)

Plantation homes in the Deep South are great places to go searching for ghosts. The genteel mansions, with welcoming porches and wide spreading front lawns, belie the fact that they were built and maintained with the sweat and tears of enslaved people. This tension, and the lingering pain of those people, have led to many hauntings across the South.

One of the most haunted of these grand homes is The Myrtles Plantation, in St. Francisville, Louisiana. The Myrtles has a rich history befitting a Southern plantation ... and plenty of ghost stories.

The home was built in 1796 by General David Bradford, and named Laurel Grove. Bradford lived there alone for several years, then sent for his wife Elizabeth and their five children, who were living in Pennsylvania. Bradford died in 1808, leaving Elizabeth to run the place.

In 1817, she relinquished the day-to-day business of the plantation to Clarke Woodrooff. (Woodrooff, one of Bradford's law students, had married David and Elizabeth's daughter Sara Mathilda, so he was brought into the family.) The Woodrooffs had three children, Cornelia Gale, James, and Mary Octavia. Sadly, the years 1823 and 1824 were rough on the family, as Sara, James, and Cornelia all perished of yellow fever.

In 1831, Clarke Woodrooff and Mary Octavia, his surviving daughter, moved away and left the plantation in the hands of a caretaker. Woodrooff sold the plantation outright in 1834—house, land, slaves and all—to Ruffin Gray Stirling and his wife, Mary Catherine Cobb Stirling. He moved to New Orleans and changed the spelling of his last name to Woodruff. (This will be important later, as it is his name that crops up in the most famous ghost story of The Myrtles.)

The Stirlings threw themselves into the welfare of the plantation, remodeling the house to almost twice its original size, and filling it with furniture imported from England. They also changed the name of the plantation to The Myrtles, as the yard was plentiful with crepe myrtle trees.

Ruffin Stirling died July 17, 1854, so he missed the plundering of The Myrtles during the Civil War. The house survived, but the fine furniture and many of the Stirlings' possessions were lost. The family's fortunes also took a nosedive after the war. Mary Stirling was known for her business acumen and her brilliant management of the properties left to her by her late husband. Unfortunately, though, the Stirlings' vast wealth was in Confederate currency, worthless after the war. In addition to The Myrtles being looted by Union soldiers, Mary's affairs suffered another blow; she had invested heavily in sugar plantations that were ravaged by the destruction of the war. Added to the financial stress was deep personal loss. Of Ruffin and Mary's nine children, only four lived long enough to marry.

Mary Stirling hired her son-in-law, William Drew Winter (married to her daughter Sarah) to manage the plantation. The Winters had to sell the plantation in 1868, but were able to buy it back two years later.

Financial woes weren't the only troubles the Winters faced. William and Sarah had six children, but lost a three-year-old daughter, Kate, to typhoid. And in 1871, tragedy struck again.

According to the January 1871 issue of the *Point Coupee Democrat*, William Winter was teaching a Sunday school lesson on January 21 in the gentlemen's parlor of The Myrtles when he heard the hoofbeats of a rider approaching on horseback. The rider called for William to come out, that he had some business with him. Suspecting nothing, William walked out onto the porch. A shot rang out, and William collapsed. Those inside the house rushed out at the sound of gunfire, but the attacker had already wheeled his horse and fled. The murderer was never caught.

A fanciful version of the story says that William dragged

himself inside and crawled up the stairs, perishing on the seventeenth step. An even more fanciful version holds that Sarah flew down the staircase and met her husband on the seventeenth step, where he died in her arms. Both of these make for delightfully creepy tales, but in reality, William died on the porch where he'd been shot.

Since the 1950s, The Myrtles has been reported to be crazy haunted. Legend has it that there were ten murders in the house, but the murder of William Winter is the only one for which we have any historical evidence. And the most famous ghost that haunts The Myrtles may never have existed at all.

Every paranormal enthusiast has heard of Chloe, the ghost of the slave woman who haunts The Myrtles. According to the stories, the tale began soon after the 1817 marriage of Sara Mathilda Bradford and Clarke Woodruff. As the story goes, Sara had given birth to two daughters, and was pregnant with her third child. Woodruff was not content to remain faithful to Sara during her pregnancies, so he forced himself on a young house slave named Chloe. Chloe submitted to Woodruff's demands only because she feared being sent out to work in the fields—labor much more strenuous than her tasks in the house.

Eventually Woodruff tired of Chloe, and turned his amorous attentions to another girl. Chloe was certain that this meant that she would be sent to the fields after all. She took to eavesdropping on the family's conversations, hoping to learn her fate. Woodruff caught her at this one day, and ordered one of her ears cut off as a reminder not to listen at doors. From that day on, Chloe wore a green turban to hide the jagged scar and the hole of her missing ear.

Chloe seethed at this punishment. She came up with a plan—although even the folks who tell this story are unclear about her motives. Chloe wanted to make the family sick, either to get her revenge, or to nurse them back to health and earn their gratitude, keeping her place in the big house.

Chloe's plan was simple. She baked a cake in honor of the Woodruffs' oldest daughter's birthday, and mixed a handful of crushed poisonous oleander leaves into the cake batter. Sara and the two girls had slices of the cake, and by the end of the day, all three were deathly ill. Chloe tried to minister to them and save them, but she had misjudged the strength of the oleander flowers. All three of them died.

The other slaves, fearing Woodruff's retribution, dragged Chloe outside and hanged her. Her body was later cut down, weighted with rocks, and thrown into the river ... a perfect recipe for a vengeful haunting.

"But, but, but ..." I hear you cry. Good! That means you've been paying attention. Sara Mathilda did have three children—and did not die while pregnant with the third one—but her two oldest were a son and a daughter, not two daughters. Neither was Sara poisoned. As mentioned earlier in this story, Sara died July 21, 1823, of yellow fever. The dreaded disease also took Sara and Clarke's son James on July 15, 1824, just shy of a year after Sara's passing. Two months later, Cornelia Gale, their oldest daughter, also succumbed to yellow fever. So the three Woodruffs did die of the same thing—it just wasn't from being poisoned by oleander. This also allows for the birth of Octavia, who was the only Woodruff child to survive. Rather than being poisoned in utero, Octavia grew up, got married, and lived to a ripe old age.

While we're at it, let's take a moment to clear Clarke Woodruff's besmirched reputation. He was not murdered, as the tale holds. Nor, it seems, did he force himself on any of the enslaved women on the plantation. He was so distraught at Sara's death that he never remarried. He died in 1851 at the plantation owned by Octavia and her husband.

And what of Chloe (or Cleo—the several versions of the story can't even agree on her name)? Does she still wander The Myrtles in her distinctive green turban?

Well ... sort of.

In the 1950s, ownership of The Myrtles passed to Marjorie Munson. She heard whispers of ghostly happenings at her new home, so she asked around for stories. (I guess she figured that any plantation worth its cotton ought to have a few ghosts floating around.) Former owners, the Williams family, used to talk about the ghost of an old woman who haunted The Myrtles. Her distinction was that she always wore a green bonnet. This moved Munson to put the Williams' family ghost in a song, in which the ghost wore a green beret. (Turban, bonnet, beret ... you can see the evolution of the ghost story.)

The Myrtles changed hands several times over the decades, and the ghost story changed and grew in response. In the 1970s, the tale evolved to incorporate the poisoned cake and the severed ear. The paranormal facet of The Myrtles really gained traction when James and Frances Myers bought the plantation. The house, when they purchased it, was filled with antiques ... and with ghost stories. Ghost hunters from all over the country soon beat a path to The Myrtles' front door.

Other stories began to crop up, like the tale of three Union soldiers who broke in and tried to loot the place. They were allegedly shot to death in the gentlemen's parlor—the parlor in which William Winter was actually leading a lesson when he was lured outside and shot—and where one of them fell, a stain in the shape of a human body was left, a stain which defied all attempts to clean it. (There is absolutely no record of Union soldiers being killed in the house, and as a matter of fact, the owners of the house claim that this particular story is untrue. Imagine someone making up ghost stories about YOUR house ...)

But the tale of Chloe persists ... and may contain a grain of truth. There is no record of any of the slaveholders at The Myrtles ever owning a woman named Chloe. However, we know that Marjorie Munson went out into the community in search of ghost stories. This may have been her reaction to experiencing some sort of weirdness in the house.

And in 1987, Frances Myers claimed that she experienced the ghost of a woman in a green turban for herself. She said that on only her second night in the house, she had a couple of terrifying encounters.

The Myrtles was being run as a bed and breakfast, and the former owner stayed on for a while to show the Myerses the ropes. There were guests staying in the 28-room mansion, so when Frances heard footsteps coming up the stairs, she didn't think anything of it. But when the doorknob started rattling, and Frances called out and didn't get an answer, she started to freak out a little. When she thought the coast was clear, she made a dash downstairs and tried to wake the owner. Unsuccessful, she calmed herself with a few nips of cherry brandy, and fell asleep on a sofa. Her sleep was interrupted again by the feeling of being watched.

She awoke to see an older Black woman wearing a long dress and a green turban. The woman was standing silently beside the sofa, holding a candlestick. The candle even gave off a soft glow. Frances shrieked in terror at the unexpected sight. When the initial shock had passed, Frances gathered the courage to take another look. The ghost was still there; in fact, she hadn't moved at all. Frances reached out a cautious hand for a touch ... and the ghost disappeared.

So there is *someone* wandering The Myrtles in a green turban, and she is seen often enough to keep the myth of Chloe alive. This ghost has even been photographed. The Myerses took a series of photos of the plantation's buildings for insurance purposes. The pictures were intended simply to show the distance between the buildings in case of fire. But one picture showed an older woman standing near one of the buildings—a woman who wasn't there when the photo was taken.

Another inadvertent capture involved a photograph of a teacher and her student taken on the porch of The Myrtles. Behind the two can be seen a window, with the translucent figure of a young girl peering out at the living. Other paranormal experiences include witnesses hearing children at play, or a piano that plays one solemn chord over and over, only stopping when someone walks into the room.

The Myrtles has a reputation for being thoroughly, solidly haunted. Even if Chloe doesn't exist, there are plenty of other spirits, including the murdered William Drew Winter, who call The Myrtles home.

The Millstadt Axe Murders (1874)

A quiet house—too quiet—still and silent in the morning air. Break-of-day chores left undone. A concerned neighbor peering in through a front window. An entire family brutally murdered, hacked with an axe as they slept.

This scenario is a perfect description of the infamous Villisca Axe Murders. Unfortunately, this scene took place hundreds of miles from Villisca, and decades before that tragedy.

On the morning of March 19, 1874, Benjamin Schneider noticed that his neighbors, the Steltzenreides, were not up and about their first chores of the day. The horses and cows penned in the front lot had not yet been watered or fed. Schneider lived near the Steltzenreides on Saxton Road, outside Millstadt in southwestern Illinois. Schneider had come to collect some seed potatoes, but as he approached the house, he could tell something was horribly wrong.

Schneider knocked on the front door, but there was no answer. He peered through the window into the darkness of the house, but no movement within caught his eye. Schneider took his courage in both hands, turned the doorknob, and pushed the door open.

Frederich Steltzenreide, aged 35, was lying in a pool of blood just inside the door. His throat was slashed, and he'd been savagely beaten, badly enough that three of his fingers had been sliced off. Frederich's wife, Anna, 28, was found dead in her bed, also with her throat cut. With her were her children, Carl, 3 years old, and 8-month-old Anna. Anna was lying across her mother's chest, her tiny arms wrapped around her mother's neck. All three of them had also been bludgeoned to death.

Carl's face was a pulpy, sodden mass of flesh, unrecognizable as human.

In the hallway lay the body of Carl Steltzenreide, the family patriarch, aged 70. He had been hacked with an axe so many times that he was nearly decapitated. His body was found sprawled on the floor in the hallway between his bedroom and the room in which the others were found. Investigators later theorized that Carl had heard an intruder come into the house, and that he had been attacked and killed as he tried to defend his family.

The only living creature in the house was the family's dog, a German shepherd named Monk. Monk was found keeping silent watch over the bodies of Anna and her children. Monk was very protective of the family, and known to be savage toward strangers. The dog's presence turned out to be a clue; the murderer had to have been someone Monk knew and trusted.

There were a couple of suspects in the vicious murders. Footprints led away from the house, along with a deep gouge in the ground, a furrow that looked like someone had been wearily dragging an axe behind him. At the end of the trail, a deputy sheriff found a half-full pouch of chewing tobacco, covered with blood. He theorized that whoever had left the trail had been wounded in the attack, and had tried an old folk remedy of packing a cut with tobacco to staunch bleeding and prevent infection. The bloody footprints led straight to the front door of Frederick Boeltz, the younger Steltzenreide's brother-in-law.

Boeltz was married to Anna Steltzenreide's sister. He had borrowed $200 from the family, and had never repaid the debt. This led to bad blood between Boeltz and his in-laws. Boeltz was arrested and tried for the murders. Astoundingly, the jury found him not guilty. Later, he sued the Steltzenreide estate for $400. He got the money, then left town and was never heard from again.

Boeltz palled around with a man named John Afken. Afken made a hardscrabble living as an itinerant farm worker, and he'd done work for the Steltzenreide family. Afken was a large, powerfully built man who swung an axe for a living. He also had a bad temper, and many people in the area feared him. He, too, had run afoul of Frederich Steltzenreide. Most interestingly, Afken had shocking bright red hair … hair that exactly matched a clump of hair Carl Steltzenreide had clutched in his cold, dead fingers as he lay in a spreading pool of his own blood.

Afken, too, was arrested and tried. Inexplicably, a jury again said that there was not enough evidence to connect him to the murders. He, too, walked free. Legend has it that after the murders, Afken took to carrying an expensive gold pocketwatch—an extravagance that seemed way out of Afken's price range … a watch very similar to one once owned by Carl Steltzenreide. Whenever anyone asked Afken where he'd gotten such an impressive piece of personal jewelry, he would simply give the questioner a serene smile.

The house in which the Steltzenreides were slaughtered no longer stands, but another house has been built on the site. And the land remembers. In 1986, Randy Eckert, a Millstadt local who grew up hearing about the murders, bought the farm and lived in the house for a couple of years.

A couple of years was enough for him.

Every year around the anniversary of the killings, Eckert and his wife would notice strange activity in the house—doors opening and closing, mysterious footsteps.

One year, the activity was very specific. Eckert and his wife were woken from sleep by the shivering and whining of their small dog. The wife said, "Do you hear something?" Eckert said he did. Suddenly the silence of the night was pierced by the ghostly howl of a dog—a dog that had lived a hundred years ago.

Then things got even stranger.

"We heard someone pounding on the door," Eckert says. "The door to the house has glass windows and it's a very small house. One step out of the bedroom and you can see the door, and that door was bounding. Somebody was beating on that door." Eckert walked to the door, keeping an eye on the window the whole time, and not seeing anyone outside. The sound faded the closer he got to the door, and by the time he reached the door, the pounding had stopped.

The Murder of the Donnelly Family (1880)

In the 1840s, many immigrants from Ireland showed up on the shores of the New World, seeking a better life for themselves and their families. The Donnellys were just more faces in the crowd of humanity that sought to improve their lot in life. But James Donnelly, his wife Johannah, and their son James Jr. traveled to Canada under a cloud. Sit down, strap in, and hang on—this one's gonna be a bumpy, complicated ride.

The shocking murders of the Donnelly family left a stain on Canadian history that hasn't faded, even in the present day. On the night of February 3, 1880, long-simmering resentments boiled over into violence. When it was over, five people were dead in two houses, one of which was in flames. How did this happen?

The story begins in Ireland in the middle of the nineteenth century (and, to be honest, about two hundred years before that, but we'll get to that in a bit). James Donnelly, a squat, stumpy stagecoach driver, fell in love with a tall, strongly built woman named Johanna Magee. Johanna's father was against this relationship, so James and Johannah eloped. Then around 1842 James went off to Canada to seek his fortune. A lot of families from Tipperary were emigrating to Biddulph Township, near Lucan in Ontario. James fetched up in London, Ontario, and started working, trying to build up enough funds to bring his new wife to the New World to join him.

Meanwhile, Johannah discovered that she was pregnant. This gave her a bit of leverage over her father, who was still ticked about the whole situation. She gave birth to a son, whom she named James Jr. She took the baby to her father and said, "Look, this kid's going to grow up without a father unless I go and find my husband. Is that what you want for your grandson?" Her father admitted that no, it wasn't, so he gave her some cash and sent her on her way. Johannah found her way to London, Ontario, and started looking for James. She found him in a bar, drinking with his buddies after a long day's work.

"Where'd YOU come from?" James sputtered.

"Where'd you GO?!?" was Johannah's retort.

The newlyweds were reunited, and started life in London. James continued to work, and in 1844 another son was born. William was born with a deformed foot, and would be known all his life by the nickname "Clubfoot Will".

City life held no appeal for James, who wanted to farm the land on which he lived, making a good honest living for his family. The Canada Land Company was offering land in Biddulph Township to Irish settlers, leasing it with an option to buy. But the Donnellys were poor folks, and James knew he could never afford to buy land.

So he squatted on 100 acres instead. He wasn't alone; it was common practice for poor people to do this, especially on the frontier. James settled on land on the Roman line near Biddulph belonging to an absentee landlord, Patrick Fogarty. (Fogarty later sold the land to John Grace, who never registered it.) He threw a shanty together and began to clear the land. Over the years, five more boys would be born to the couple: John, Patrick, Michael, Robert, and Thomas. James made improvements to the shanty, turning it into a cozy cabin. All went fairly well until 1855, when John Grace (you know, the rightful owner of the property) sold the southern 50 acres of his land to Michael Maher for 200 pounds.

James was furious at the impending loss of "his" land. He'd worked hard clearing that land, and he felt he deserved to be able to stay on it. He dared anyone to take the southern fifty acres from him. Surprisingly, no one challenged him.

No one, that is, except a man named Patrick Farrell.

In 1857, Farrell had rented the land from Michael Maher, the

Sylvia Shults

new absentee owner. But when he showed up to claim the land, James told him to go pound sand. They went to court over the dispute. The court ruled a tradeoff: James was actually allowed to keep the northern fifty acres of the property. But he had to give up the southern half to Farrell. No one knew it yet, but the court had just made a decision that would change Biddulph's history forever.

On June 25, 1857, William Maloney hosted a logging bee. Bees were very common in pioneer days. Going on the maxim "many hands make light work", they were a way for neighbors to help each other with tasks that needed attention. There were logging bees, quilting bees, corn-shucking bees, and barn-raising bees. These were also opportunities for socializing and, of course, drinking.

James Donnelly and Patrick Farrell were both invited to this logging bee, and they both showed up. The booze had been flowing, and most of the farmers were tipping the bottle. So it's not really clear how the fight started—but everyone there knew that Donnelly and Farrell detested each other. Words were exchanged, which led to violence. Farrell threw a punch; James jabbed back, then decided Farrell wasn't worth his time. He turned his back and started to walk away. Farrell grabbed up a tool called a handspike, a heavy chunk of metal bigger than a railroad spike, and went after James again. Donnelly grabbed one too, to defend himself. Moments later, Patrick Farrell was lying on the ground, with a handspike jammed into his left temple. He died two days later.

James Donnelly was now a murderer. A warrant was issued for his arrest, but when constables showed up at the Donnelly farm, James was nowhere to be found. He stayed hidden for the next eleven months. No one had any idea where he was … except for Johannah and their three oldest sons. Officers showed up to the farm on the regular, trying to find James to arrest him. But the Donnellys weren't talking.

As it turned out, James had been hiding in plain sight, on his own homestead all along. Sharp-eyed observers might have noticed another woman working the Donnelly fields; they might have, but they didn't. James had disguised himself in his wife's dresses so as to be able to work next to her in their fields without attracting too much attention. He spent time hidden in the houses of sympathetic neighbors—and some time in his own house too: their final child, a girl named Jennie, was born at this time. But winters in Ontario are bitterly cold, and after spending one of them sleeping in stables or sheltered in the homes of sympathetic friends, James decided not to spend another one outdoors. In August 1858, James turned himself in.

James hired one of the best lawyers in the province, but even so, he was found guilty, and sentenced to death by hanging. The execution was set for September 17, 1859.

Johannah was devastated by the news, but she was not about to lose her beloved husband, and see her children left fatherless, without a fight. She started up a petition for a lighter sentence, and she had people sign it everywhere she went. Johannah was very well-respected in the community: she started up a school for neighborhood children on their homestead, and was well-known for her love of kids. (Perhaps having seven of her own helped.) In addition to that, after Patrick Farrell's death, Johannah and James took in Farrell's son, adopted him, and raised him as their own. In July 1859, her persistence paid off. In the London Free Press account of that day it is reported that Patrick Farrell had attacked James Donnelly with his fists. James defended himself with his fists and knocked Farrell down, then was walking away when Farrell picked up a logging handspike and attacked James from behind. James then defended himself with another handspike and Farrell was killed. This is why the hanging sentence was commuted on appeal, because the death was self defense. Instead of being hanged, he was sentenced to seven years in Kingston Penitentiary. He was released in 1865.

He came home to a houseful of wild boys. Without the guiding hand of a father, his sons were, to tell the truth, running loose. Johannah had her hands full trying to keep them in line, raise Jennie, and keep the homestead going. Fortunately, the boys were now old enough to start finding jobs. All of the Donnelly boys were handsome, astute in business, unafraid to get into a fight, and notorious womanizers—which didn't help their reputation in the community. (All the boys, except for Will, were scrappers. James Jr. died at the age of 36; rumors were that he had been shot. And Michael was killed in a bar fight at the age of 29.)

In May 1873, William Donnelly started up a stagecoach business. "Clubfoot Will" was generally agreed to be the smartest of the Donnelly brothers. Will drew on his father's stagecoach experience from Ireland, and the Donnelly stagecoach line was soon a roaring success. Brothers Will, Michael, John, and Thomas operated the line, which ran between Lucan, Exeter, and London, Ontario. It soon began to rival the government mail stage, which had started in 1838.

The Donnellys' rival for the stage business was the Hawkshaw line, which soon began to crumble under pressure from the competition. In October 1873, Hawkshaw knuckled under and sold his business to Patrick Flanagan. Flanagan was determined to run his fellow Irishmen out of business.

The Stagecoach Feud, between the Donnelly Stagecoach and the Flanagan & Crawly Stage, erupted in Biddulph, sweeping the area with violence. Coaches were smashed, wrecked, and burned, stables were torched, and horses were savagely beaten and even killed. The Donnellys somehow got the blame for most of this violence, and the family began to get a bad reputation.

Here's one example of many: in 1875, one of Flanagan's stages was destroyed and stage driver William Brooks was killed when a wheel fell off. It was assumed by all that the accident was a result of sabotage. Robert McLeod, who worked for Flanagan, cut off the Donnelly stage on the road, causing passengers to fall out of the carriage. Will Donnelly charged him, and received damages. The passengers, Louisa and Martha Lindsay, turned around and charged the Donnellys for dumping them out of the stage, and the Donnellys were forced to pay damages to them.

The anger generated by the Stagecoach Feud spread, and soon the Donnellys were being accused of everything from trespassing to assaulting a police officer to attempted murder. This all makes them sound like a bunch of jerks, but these types of crime were normal for frontier communities. It's just that the Donnellys got blamed for *everything*. According to a contemporary newspaper account, if a housewife left a pie to cool on her porch, and a dog stole it, the Donnellys would get blamed. And it wasn't just the Donnelly men who were accused. Johannah would quite often swear a blue streak at police constables, especially Constable James Carroll.

Unfortunately, feuds like this were a way of life in Biddulph. The Roman line, the main road through the area, which ran right past the Donnelly farmhouse, was named for the Roman Catholics who settled in Biddulph. The Biddulph feud had begun in Ireland some two centuries before James Donnelly was born. Biddulph was settled mainly by Irish immigrants, who brought the long-standing bitterness between Catholics and Protestants with them to the New World.

Things really began to heat up in June 1879. Father John Connolly, pastor of St. Patrick's Catholic Church, created a "Peace Society" in Biddulph. He asked members of his congregation to sign a pledge of support, which included an agreement to let society members search their homes for stolen property. The Donnellys did not sign the pledge. (Fr. Connolly didn't like the Donnellys anyway. He came to the community and heard the horror stories before he met the family for himself. He formed a bad opinion of them right from the jump. Will wrote to him to explain that his family wasn't all that bad, and that the priest should give them a fair shake, but Fr. Connolly was unmoved in his prejudice.)

James was quite liberal—he even donated money to help build an Anglican church, which did not endear him to Fr. Connolly or the Peace Society. One Sunday, though, Fr. Connolly really ticked James off. The Catholic priest was in the pulpit preaching hatred against Protestants. The Donnellys had many Protestant friends. James stood up in the middle of Mass, denounced Connolly for his unChristian attitude, and proclaimed that from then on, he and his family would attend the Catholic church in London.

In August 1879, a splinter group of the Peace Society, also organized by Fr. Connolly, started meeting in Biddulph. They called themselves the Vigilance Committee, and they really had it in for the Donnellys. They met regularly at the Cedar Swamp Schoolhouse—incidentally, the same school for which Johannah had provided the land.

Not long after the Vigilance Committee was formed, a cow went missing from the farm of William and Mary Thompson, a Black couple. The Vigilance Committee immediately accused the Donnellys of the theft, and searched the farm for the missing cow. Constable James Carroll led the search. The cow was later found at the Thompson's farm, right where she belonged. The Donnellys accused the Vigilance Committee of trespassing. Back and forth, back and forth …

The spark that touched off the final confrontation came on January 15, 1880. Patrick "Grouchy" Ryder's barn burned down. Everyone—spurred on by the Peace Society—blamed the Donnellys. (Actually, some of the incidents of arson, property damage and violence in Biddulph at the time were in fact the work of the Peace Society.) There was absolutely no evidence that pointed to the Donnellys being the arsonists, and all of the Donnelly boys had been at a wedding the night the barn burned. So James and Johannah were blamed. Ryder himself said that he'd been neighbor to the Donnellys for over thirty years and had never had an issue with them, and that the only reason he sent constables after them was that they were regularly blamed for everything.

Father Connolly stepped up to the pulpit at St. Patrick's and spoke to his congregation. He said that an evil had fallen on the community, and that $500 would be offered as a reward for getting rid of the wicked. Since there was zero evidence linking the Donnellys to the burning of Grouchy Ryder's barn, members of the community decided to take the law into their own hands.

On the morning of February 3, James Donnelly sat down at the kitchen table with his son Tom, and with Tom's help drafted a letter to his lawyer regarding the Ryder arson case. The Donnellys were expected in court the next day. James wrote to the lawyer outlining the facts of the case: Grouchy had been their neighbor for thirty years and they'd never had any trouble, and there was no evidence to suggest that he and Johannah had set the fire. He added, "It seems hard to see a man and woman over 60 years of age dragged around as laughingstock."

The day went on as usual, with James Jr., John, and Tom leaving around 4 pm to pick up a neighbor boy, Johnny

O'Connor. Johnny often helped the Donnellys with farm chores, and it was not unusual for him to come and stay with the family. This time, Johnny was to care for the pigs while the family was in Granton for the court appearance.

When they got back to the house, John and Tom put the horse away, then John left to visit Will, who lived at Whalen's Corners. Johnny fed the pigs and did more chores in the barn. Around 10 pm, a neighbor, Jim Feeheley, stopped in to say hello, but didn't stay long. Then everyone settled down for the night.

The Donnelly house was small, so Johnny bunked with James in the front bedroom. Johanna slept in her own room, sharing her bed with Bridget, her niece, who was visiting from Ireland. Tom had his own bed in a little room off the kitchen.

Just after midnight on February 4, members of the Vigilance Committee gathered at the Cedar Swamp Schoolhouse to get all liquored up before heading out to the Donnelly homestead. The group included Grouchy Ryder, whose barn had been torched, and James Carroll, one of the constables Johannah Donnelly was known to swear at. In all, 35 men showed up at the Donnelly home that night, thirsting for blood. Jim Feeheley's earlier visit had really been a scouting trip, to see where each Donnelly was in the house. (He didn't notice Johnny O'Connor, so the boy's presence went unreported.)

James Carroll came quietly into the house, took handcuffs out of his pocket, and handcuffed Tom Donnelly while Tom was still asleep. Then he woke Tom up and told him he was under arrest. Things escalated very quickly from that point. Carroll frog-marched Tom into the kitchen. Johannah and Bridget woke up and came into the kitchen too. James Sr. soon joined them from his bedroom, asking Carroll "What have you got against us now?" Carroll responded that more charges were being filed against them. James noticed the handcuffs on Tom, and asked, "You are handcuffed?"

"Yes," Tom replied, nodding at Carroll, "he thinks he's smart." Then, as if taunting Carroll further, Tom demanded, "Read the warrant."

They were the last words he would ever speak.

At a signal from Carroll, the men outside stormed the house.

They were all armed with sticks, clubs, and various farm tools, and they began beating the three adults. Bridget broke free and ran upstairs. Johnny, unnoticed by the attackers, slipped out of bed and followed her up the stairs, but Bridget didn't notice him either, and inadvertently slammed the door in his face. Johnny fled back down the stairs and hid under the bed in the front bedroom, where he'd been sleeping.

James Donnelly was the first to fall; the men beat him in the head, pulping his skull. Johannah was also bludgeoned to death. Tom, only 25 years old and strong, fought hard to protect himself and his family. He made it just outside the front door, where Tom Ryder was waiting for him with a pitchfork. He savaged Tom Donnelly, stabbing him in the chest with the sharp tines over and over. Once Tom was down, the men carried him back into the kitchen where his parents' bodies lay, and took the handcuffs off him. Tom was still alive, and groaning. Someone said, "Hit that fellow on the head and break his skull open." One of the men, either Jim Toohey or Patrick Quigley, bashed Tom's head with a shovel three or four times.

The men realized that Bridget Donnelly was missing. They found her upstairs, and killed the 21-year-old girl too. The Donnellys' dog wouldn't stop barking at all the commotion, so one of the men smashed the dog's head with a shovel, killing it.

Then they went to the front bedroom, poured coal oil all over the bed under which Johnny lay quivering with terror, and lit the bed on fire, hoping that the whole house would soon catch.

Then the men went hunting for more Donnellys.

Will Donnelly lived with his wife Nora in Whalen's Corners, not far from the Donnelly homestead. On the night of February 3, he and Nora had two visitors, brother John, and Martin Hogan, a friend. John was there to borrow a sleigh for the ride into Granton for court the next day, and Martin had just come for a visit. Martin and John were both invited to stay the night. Nora went to bed around 9 pm, and the men stayed up talking, finally turning in around 12:30.

Nora was about six months pregnant at the time, and not feeling her best. When Will came in to bed, he asked Nora to roll over next to the wall, so he could get into bed more easily. She sleepily protested, saying she didn't want to leave her warm spot. So Will climbed over her. That small concession to Nora's comfort probably saved Will's life.

Will had been asleep for about two hours when he was woken up by John coming through his bedroom on the way to the kitchen and back door. Will groggily registered that someone outside was yelling his name and shouting about fire. "Fire! Fire! Open the door, Will!"

Actually, this wasn't a warning; it was a ploy to get Will to come outside to be shot. The mob had thrown away all pretense of stealth at that point. They were out for Will's blood; he was considered the smartest of the Donnelly brothers, and the mob wanted him dead. They surrounded the house, but instead of storming inside, they tried to get Will to come out. They broke into the barn and led Will's prize stallion out, and started beating it savagely, hoping that the horse's screams would draw Will out of the house.

But it was John who opened the door—and was cut down by several blasts from a shotgun. John dropped with thirty holes in his chest and groin. The shots pierced his lung and broke his collarbone and several ribs. Nora tried to move John to safety, but he was too heavy for her to drag. Martin helped her drag John to the bedroom, where Nora forced his hand closed around a piece of blessed candle. John, just 32 years old, died within five minutes of being shot.

After milling around for a while longer, the mob drifted away. Will, Nora, and Martin huddled on the floor next to John's cooling body until the dawn broke.

Meanwhile, the Donnelly cabin continued to burn. Johnny had wriggled out from under the bed as soon as the mob left, and ran to Patrick Whalen's cabin next door. Whalen took the boy in, but warned him not to speak of the killings. The Donnelly cabin was soon engulfed in flames. The second floor collapsed, sending Bridget's body tumbling into the kitchen to join the others. Falling snow eventually covered the crime scene, snuffing the flames. Investigators later piled the charred remains of all four Donnellys into one coffin for the funeral service.

Will and Nora Donnelly and Martin Hogan all recognized the men who had killed John Donnelly. (One of them was John Kennedy, Nora's brother.) And young Johnny O'Connor witnessed the whole horrible scene at the Donnelly farmhouse. Will and Patrick Donnelly spent all their time leading up to the trial searching the community for more witnesses. But no one was ever punished for the two-part massacre, despite Johnny's court testimony. The authorities in Biddulph simply covered the whole thing up.

Eventually, six men were tried for the Donnelly murders: James Carroll, the constable who ran afoul of Johannah, John Purtell, Thomas Ryder (Grouchy's brother), James Ryder, Jr., Martin McLaughlin, and John Kennedy (Will's brother-in-law). All of the men backed up each other's alibis. One juror said that he wouldn't have convicted even if he'd seen the murders done himself. Another didn't want to convict just on the testimony of a twelve-year-old boy. The rest were afraid of the defendants: the press was pretty firmly on Will and Patrick's side, and described Carroll and the others as "a bunch of envious, dangerous backwoodsmen." The first trial ended with a hung jury: seven to acquit, four to convict, and one undecided.

In the second trial, James Carroll was tried first—the prosecutor figured that if he was convicted, there was a better chance of getting more convictions down the line. Carroll had been the first one into the Donnelly cabin, and he stood accused of the murders of James and Johannah. Johnny O'Connor was called to the stand to testify, but his eyewitness testimony was largely ignored. His mother was also called. But the defense argued that Johnny's mother had asked the court for money, and therefore her testimony was suspect, as was her son's. (They conveniently ignored the fact that Johnny's mother had, indeed, asked for money … because their house had been burned down in retribution for their court appearance. They really did need the help.) James Carroll walked away from the trial a free man. Without his conviction, there was no reason to try the other five men, and they were released on bail.

The surviving Donnellys were incredibly magnanimous towards some of the people involved in their family's murder.

Will and Patrick befriended Jim Feeheley, who scouted out the cabin that fateful night. He confessed to Patrick the part he'd played in the evening's gruesome events. He said he was afraid of the Vigilance Committee. In April 1881, Jim and Michael Feeheley fled to Michigan, but were extradited back to Canada in September and charged with aiding and abetting the murder of Tom Donnelly. They refused to testify against anyone, so the prospect of a third trial fizzled out. The Crown agreed to let them go on bail, which was paid for by—wait for it—the Vigilance Committee.

The Donnelly property still bears the psychic imprint of the ghastly crime. The paranormal activity on the land is extreme. Horses seem to be especially sensitive to the psychic residue. Horses ridden near the property late at night on February 3 will refuse to go any further, or go berserk as if possessed. If they are forced to go any further after balking, the horses soon die mysteriously. This has happened to at least three mounts.

The weirdness doesn't stop with the doomed horses. Blue balls of lightning have been seen rolling down the road next to the Donnelly land on the anniversary of the killings. Photographs of the Donnelly tombstones on the property show strange figures and light anomalies.

Robert and Linda Salts moved into the Donnelly house in 1988, and experienced paranormal activity from the very first day. The original house no longer stands, of course. In 1881, a year after the massacre, some of the surviving family members, sons Will, James Jr., Patrick, and Robert, restored the middle part of the house. The rest of the house was built around this.

The Salts family hear footsteps going up the stairs late at night, and shadowy figures move through the house constantly. The ghosts of James and Johannah are dressed austerely in somber black, while the spirits of the Donnelly sons appear in white clothes. Will's ghost can sometimes be seen in the yard behind the house, as that was a favorite place of his.

Even the barn, built in 1877, is haunted. Tourists visiting the barn have experienced a heavy feeling pressing down on their chests. Visitors have also reported phantom footsteps, and, more chillingly, the sound of screams.

People in Ontario still speak in whispers of the Donnelly murders. It's been 140 years, and the crime was so heinous that it still reverberates today. Add to that the fact that the murderers, although well-known to all, were never brought to justice, and you have a story that deserves to live on in infamy.

Double Double Blood and Trouble
or
The Face(s) on the Gravestone(s) (1893, early 1900s)

When a historic event develops into a ghost story, or an inexplicable occurrence leads to an explanation with a whiff of the paranormal, things can sometimes get … a little complicated.

Take the story of Olga and Heinrich Schultz, for example. The elderly couple lived in Cherokee County in Iowa, near the town of Washta, in the early 1900s. Heinrich found that he needed some temporary help bringing in his harvest of hay, so he hired a drifter named Will Florence. Heinrich and Olga were well liked in the community, and Heinrich's neighbors told him flatly that they didn't trust the sullen stranger. Florence had drifted into the area some time before, in search of work. Most of Heinrich's neighbors, not liking the looks of the fellow, had sent him on his way. But Heinrich had a generous heart, and he hated to see anyone down on their luck. He hired Florence, even providing him with room and board in addition to his wages.

Florence was no one's idea of a model employee. He was tight-lipped about his past. He told Heinrich that he'd had experience with outdoorsy-type work, but Heinrich found him clumsy and awkward with even the simplest farm chores. Nevertheless, true to his patient nature, the older man walked

Florence through the tasks expected of him.

One afternoon, Heinrich heard through the grapevine that the bank in town was edging towards failure. The Great Depression was a couple of decades in the future, but even at that time, banks were going under with worrisome frequency. Heinrich decided to err on the side of caution. Leaving Olga at home, he headed into Washta to withdraw his money. He figured the cash would be safer hidden away in his mattress or in a Mason jar in the backyard than it would be in a teetering bank.

Three days later, the Schultzes' neighbors realized that no one had seen or heard from the couple in several days. A friend came by to check on them, opened the front door, and walked into a scene from a horror movie.

Heinrich and Olga were lying in the kitchen in a huge pool of blood. Their heads had been split open with an axe. The house was ransacked, the money that Heinrich had withdrawn from his bank account was missing ... and so was Will Florence.

Florence was tracked down a few days later in Nebraska. He was arrested and taken back to Iowa. The prosecutor in Washta really wanted to indict Florence for the murder of the Schultzes, and dragged the vagrant in front of a grand jury. However, there just wasn't enough evidence to get an indictment, let alone a conviction. Will Florence was released, and left town in a hurry.

Heinrich and Olga Schultz were laid to rest in the cemetery in Washta. As friends and neighbors paid their respects at the grave over the next few weeks, they began to notice something strange about the gravestone that marked the elderly couple's final resting place. A stain was beginning to form on the stone—a stain that, if you squinted, sort of looked a little bit like the face of Will Florence.

People really wanted—needed—someone to blame for the senseless double murder. The concerned citizens of Washta finally convinced two police detectives to take a look at the stone. The "face" on the gravestone had become even clearer by then, and people generally agreed that it did look like the accused murderer. Maybe the Schultzes were trying to prove that Will Florence was the one who'd done them in.

The detectives couldn't arrest Florence again simply based on a weird-looking stain, but they agreed that the case could stand a closer look. They reopened the case, and discovered new evidence that investigators had missed the first time around. The fresh evidence pointed solidly to Will Florence as the killer, and the authorities issued a warrant for his arrest.

But Will Florence had disappeared for good this time. Maybe he, too, had heard of the face on the gravestone. At any rate, he went to ground more thoroughly than he had done before. He was never brought to justice for the murder of Heinrich and Olga Schultz.

The stone, though, remained as a mute witness to his guilt.

There's also the story of Martin and Helena Schultz. Martin and his wife were both natives of Germany who emigrated to the United States. Martin Schultz was born October 25, 1833, in Prussia. Helena Katherina Montagne was born in Oldenburg, Germany, on April 1, 1845. Little is known about Martin's life before he married Lena, but we know that the Montagnes came to America in 1845. They arrived via the Gulf Coast, not the East Coast, and settled in Texas for six years. In 1851, the family returned to Germany, and Lena's mother passed away. In 1863, Lena's father came back to America, and his children joined him a year later. Helena married Martin Schultz, and they began farming.

In the 1870s, John and George Montagne both bought land in Cherokee County, Iowa. In 1880, they invited their sister and brother-in-law to join them there. Martin and Lena moved to Cherokee County in 1880, taking Lena's brothers up on their offer. They were fiercely independent, living alone in a small house in Tilden Township, a mile from any neighbors. They rented eighty acres from Lena's brother John. He and Helena's other brother, George Montagne Sr., were both wealthy landowners.

The Schultzes had that dream for themselves, too. They socked away every cent they made, in the hope of buying the land they farmed. The couple spent little on themselves, and kept their savings in their house rather than trusting a bank. Banks at that time, in the last decade of the nineteenth century, were notorious for being unstable. Runs on banks, where people suddenly withdrew all their savings in a panic, causing the bank to fail, were common. Rumor had it that the couple had over a thousand dollars in cash hidden in their house.

And this was quite an accomplishment, especially for the Schultzes. Helena, who went by the diminutive "Lena", was herself diminutive. In fact, she was listed in the 1890 census as "a hunchback" who suffered from "spinal complaint". Martin wasn't a big guy, either. The Cedar Rapids *Gazette* later wrote that "[both were] below the average size, the old lady being a deformed cripple and no more than four feet in height." So running their own eighty-acre farm can't have been easy. But they made it work. They had kind, helpful neighbors, and they had each other.

Their quiet life together came to a gruesome end. On the morning of August 17, 1893, neighbor Nick Halk came to one of Martin's fields to help stack grain. But Martin didn't show up. Halk went to the house and knocked on the front door. There was no answer, so he went around to the back of the house.

The scene that met his eyes in the back yard was one of sheer butchery. Lena lay at the corner of the house, six feet from the summer kitchen door, which stood ajar. Her head was a gory mess. Her face and skull were a ruin of savage blows. She'd been struck so hard with the murder weapon that six of her teeth were scattered on the blood-soaked ground.

Investigators determined that Lena had been killed the night before, just before dusk, when there was still enough light to move around the farmyard. She had been carrying a water dipper, so she'd been on her way either to or from the well. In the kitchen was a lump of fresh butter that Lena had taken from the churn just before heading out to the well. (When a housewife churns cream into butter, the newly-made butter has to be washed in cool water to get the last of the buttermilk out, or it will go sour.)

The horror continued in the house. Martin lay in a small bedroom, his head split open with gashes two inches deep, his face pulped beyond recognition. His left arm was bruised and cut with defensive wounds. The floor was sticky with congealed blood, and bloody fingerprints smeared the handle of the door between the bedroom and the sitting room. Near Martin's body was a hammer, covered in blood and brains.

The coroner's jury, convened the same day, ruled that Lena and Martin had been murdered with a blunt instrument. Authorities didn't yet have a suspect, but they reasoned it was probably someone who knew the Schultzes—and knew that they had a secret stash of cash. The killer ransacked the house looking for the money, but investigators were unsure of how much had been stolen, as they had no idea how much had been hidden in the first place. It was determined that between $250 and $300 was missing from a deerskin pocketbook. But the intruder missed $5.45 tucked into an old Bible and $2.55 squirreled away in a baking powder can on the second floor.

By August 20, neighbors had gathered up about $1,000, a reward for the capture of the killer. The Cherokee County Board of Supervisors kicked in another $500, and Iowa governor Horace Boles offered enough to bring the total to an even $2,000.

And so the hunt began. In mid-September, 30-year-old Jack Skinner was arrested in Sioux City for the murders. It was reported that Skinner had been seen skulking around outside the Schultz farmhouse on the night of the killings. Witnesses also said that Skinner, a generally unsavory character, was broke before the murders, but seemed to have plenty of spending money afterwards.

Skinner was clapped into the Cherokee County jail to await his grand jury trial. Sheriff Dan Unger was so concerned that public fury at the crime would lead to Skinner's being lynched that he stationed an extra guard on Skinner's cell. But there was no evidence to link Skinner to the crime, so he was released on October 11.

Pinkerton operatives were called in to investigate the case. They picked up several local bad types, including Will Florence, but the suspects were all released when no evidence could be found for their guilt.

Despite the sizeable reward, authorities could not come up with suspects in the crime and make the charges stick. It began to look as though Lena and Martin's killer would never be found.

Two years after the murders, though, it seemed that there was a break in the case. But instead of bringing jubilation, the news was deeply disconcerting. Lena's own brother, George Montagne Sr., was arrested on November 10, 1895, for the murder of his sister and brother-in-law. An informant had said that he'd heard George Sr. confess to the crime on three different occasions. This was unbelievable ... and nobody believed it. He was soon cleared and released.

Six years after *that*, on September 6, 1901, George Montagne Jr., Lena's 27-year-old nephew, told Sheriff John Hill that he had helped his father and uncle—George Sr. and John Montagne— kill the Schultzes. This news was greeted with skepticism—the community had been spoofed before—but County Attorney J.A. Miller took the man's detailed confession.

George Jr. claimed that he'd driven the two older men to the Schultz farm, and that he'd held the reins of the horses, standing with them under the shade of a tree while the others killed his aunt and uncle. He said they had taken the stashed money and had given him $80, which he stuffed into a tin can and buried under a tree.

Then he took it all back.

The whole confession was a joke, he said. Miller called his bluff and brought him before a grand jury. George Jr. then made his confession—he had indeed been involved in the murder of his aunt and uncle, and it was his father, George Sr., and his uncle John who were the killers.

Then he took it back again. Nope, it was just a joke.

That's when Miller remembered that in July 1900, the Insanity Commission had found George Jr. to be insane, and had committed him to a state asylum. He'd been released after treatment and sent home. Miller brought George Jr. before the Commission again. This time, the members found him not insane, only "simple".

Miller also discovered that George Jr. was harboring a grudge against his father. He'd thought he was going to be given a quarter section of the family farm when he turned 27, but it hadn't happened. So George Jr. refused to do any farm work at all until he got his land, and just loafed around (and made up lies about his father killing his relatives).

Investigators realized that their potential lead was quite possibly mentally ill, and most certainly seeking attention and revenge. They couldn't consider George Jr.'s testimony with any seriousness.

Another possible suspect popped up in March of 1899. Martha Nellis, a former Cherokee County resident living in South Dakota, told the police that her husband Oscar Nellis had killed Martin and Lena Schultz.

Her story was this: in 1893, she and Oscar had been living on a farm about a mile from the Schultzes. They'd heard the rumors that the couple had squirreled away money in order to buy the land they were currently renting. Martha said that on the night of August 16, 1893, they'd gone to bed around 9 pm, but that Oscar got up around 10 pm and got dressed, saying, "I am going over to rob those Schultzes. They've got some money and I want it." She said she tried to talk Oscar out of his plan, without success.

According to Martha's story, Oscar came back later saying that he had killed Lena when she woke up and caught him robbing the house. He left, then realized that Martin would be able to identify him, so he went back and killed Martin as well.

A week after the murders, the Nellises moved west, first to Oklahoma, then settling in South Dakota. Martha claimed that for six years, she'd been simmering in guilt and fear, as Oscar had threatened to kill her if she told anyone what he'd done.

Martha said she'd heard rumors that another woman was going to claim she'd been married to the man who had killed Martin and Lena Schultz, and so collect the $2,000 reward. Martha said that as she herself knew that wasn't true, she wanted to prevent this other woman from claiming the reward under false pretenses.

Sheriff Hill and Yankton sheriff W.M. Hickey arrested Nellis in Lodi, South Dakota, and took him back to Cherokee County. He was later sent to the Woodbury County Jail in Sioux City. Nellis said, though, that he had nothing to hide. He had an alibi for the night of the murder. On April 10, 1899, the preliminary hearing in the matter of Nellis' guilt or innocence was ended, and the case against him was dismissed.

Lena and Martin Schultz were laid to rest in Mount Pleasant Cemetery in Quimby, Iowa. The cemetery was tended by groundskeeper John Williams. Williams became obsessed with the granite headstone that marked the couple's final resting place. He swore to anyone who would listen that a picture was forming on the side of the headstone ... a stain on the granite that looked like the faces of Lena and Martin, complete with the ghastly wounds of their violent deaths.

The community ran with this, although many had a different interpretation of the discoloration on the stone. Many people believed there was only one face forming in the stain, and that when the development was complete, it would reveal the identity of the person who had murdered the Schultzes.

The stonemason who had carved the stone tried to settle the matter. He had made the gravestone out of half of a slab of Vermont granite, and he brought the other half out and put it on display. He said that in his opinion, the natural striations in the stone looked like dogs or cats, not human faces. But people stuck to their original interpretations. As time passed, and the face, or faces, didn't get any clearer (and no one was found guilty of the murders), people grudgingly admitted that maybe, the marks were just discolorations in the stone after all.

But human nature being what it is, the whole affair now had the mysterious allure of the paranormal about it. Neighbors started claiming that the Schultz house was haunted, with unexplained lights moving between the darkened rooms at night.

So what's going on here? The website for Find A Grave only has records for Lena (Helena) and Martin Schultz. Putting "Olga and Heinrich Schultz" into Google only results in a retelling of this story. Both couples were farm folk, people of the land. Olga and Heinrich were "elderly", while Lena and Martin were younger—Martin was 60 when he was murdered, hardly elderly, and Lena was only 48.

Both couples, if indeed there were two couples, were savagely murdered. The crime(s) resulted in two remarkably similar paranormal occurrences. And what about Will Florence, who seems to have a connection to both double murders? Is he the missing link here? Or is he just mentioned in both stories?

And, come to that, *are* there two stories?

Lena and Martin were killed August 17, and lore holds that Heinrich hired Will Florence to help with the haying—which happens in mid-August. Lena and Martin's grave is marked by a granite headstone, while Olga and Heinrich are purportedly honored with a stone made of marble. One stone showed the face of the alleged killer, while the other displayed the murdered couple.

Washta, where Olga and Heinrich were supposed to have lived, and Quimby, where Lena and Martin are actually buried, are only about five miles apart in Cherokee County. Maybe in the retelling, people got their places mixed up. Schultz is not an uncommon surname (I should know). But here we have "Lena and Martin" and "Olga and Heinrich", and not, say, "Leah and Marvin". Why are the names of the two couples so obviously different?

We may never know. The only thing certain is that we have not one, but two stories of gruesome death ... and telltale gravestones.

The Portal to Hell (1896)

On January 31, 1896, a music student from rural Indiana got off the train in Cincinnati, Ohio. Pearl Bryan was 22 years old, young, pretty … and five months pregnant. She was in Ohio to get an abortion. The two men who met her at the train station—her boyfriend, Scott Jackson, and his roommate, Alonzo Walling—had promised to help her.

But things didn't turn out as planned. No one really knows what happened next. Jackson and Walling swore they had taken Pearl to a doctor, who botched the procedure. Others say that the men, who were both dental students, drugged Pearl and tried to perform the abortion themselves.

In any case, Pearl Bryan was still alive when Jackson and Walling cut her head off.

The men carried the unconscious girl across the Ohio River and into the forests of northern Kentucky. They severed her neck at the fifth vertebra and left her body in the woods. Authorities later identified Pearl, but only because she'd been wearing custom-made shoes. Jackson and Walling were caught, tried, convicted, and hanged.

Pearl's head was never found.

So how does a haunting fit into this sordid little tale? We'll get to that, I promise.

You may well ask, where did Jackson and Walling get rid of poor Pearl's head? They cut it off, of course, to make identification of her body more difficult. (Obviously, they overlooked her shoes.) They had the foresight to carry the head well away from the body. True-crime enthusiasts theorize that the men took Pearl's head to a nearby slaughterhouse. The killing factory had been built in 1850, and had closed in 1890. But the building remained active, in a creepy, lowlife, things-done-in-the-dark-of-night way. Jackson and Walling had a brilliant idea to solve their head disposal problem.

In the basement of the slaughterhouse, there was a well, nothing more than a simple hole in the floor, into which workers dumped blood and offal. The gory by-products of butchery were cleaned up by nature: the well drained into the nearby Licking River. The men likely took advantage of this handy way to dispose of a human body part, sending it down the hole to join the countless buckets of animal guts that had been swilled into the well over four decades of use. Local legend says that Walling and Jackson performed some sort of occult ritual, then threw the head down the well. Some people with vivid imaginations say that this sacrilegious act created a portal to Hell. (Local legend also claims that the men were by no means the only ones performing blood rituals there. It's said that Satanists broke into the building after it had been abandoned, and used the well for their own dark rites.)

In the 1930s, the slaughterhouse was torn down. A new building was built, an establishment called the Primrose, which functioned as a roadhouse, speakeasy, and casino all rolled into one. Buck Brady owned the Primrose, and took pride in the quality of his hospitality. Unfortunately, though, the success of the Primrose attracted the attention of the Chicago mob. They moved in on the action, taking the club for themselves. Brady was heartbroken at the loss of his beloved club, and committed suicide in the Primrose to make his feelings perfectly clear.

The Mob renamed the club, and the Primrose became the Latin Quarter. There is a tragedy associated with this incarnation of the building too. A young dancer named Johanna worked at the Latin Quarter, and fell in love with a singer at the casino named Robert Randall. Their relationship ended up with Johanna falling pregnant. When her father learned of the pregnancy, he had Randall killed. (Daddy was a mobster, and they tend to solve problems with permanent solutions like that.) On learning that her father had murdered her boyfriend, Johanna took her horrific revenge. She poisoned herself, and some stories say she poisoned Daddy Dearest too. Her suicide cast yet another stain on the establishment. Some say her lifeless body was found in the dressing room of the Latin Quarter—and others claim it was found next to the old slaughterhouse well in the basement, further cementing the well's reputation as a portal to Hell.

(In the interest of historical accuracy, I'm going to interject here and point out that the veracity of this particular story is doubtful. The problem with this romantic tale is that no self-respecting mobster would allow his little girl to dance in a club that he owned. So this story is probably an embellishment, yet another facet in the events leading up to the haunting of this building.)

The Latin Quarter closed in the 1950s, and the nightclub morphed yet again. This time, it became a biker bar, a real bucket-of-blood dive known for random acts of senseless violence. The Hard Rock Cafe (don't laugh, seriously, that's what it was called) was shut down in the 1970s after a series of fatal shootings.

And in 1978, the building changed hands yet again. It became a country music club, and the owner himself often performs on stage. He is devoted to his craft, and his audience appreciates his love of music, because they share it. In fact, the building is named for the owner. It's now, according to the website, "a nightclub with live country music, line dancing, a mechanical bull, and regular ghost tours". This nonchalant description of the club belies that fact that it is one of the places on many a ghost hunter's bucket list. The name conjures thrills for country music lovers, and chills for devotees of the paranormal.

This club, Bobby Mackey's Music World, is known as one of the most viciously haunted buildings in the United States.

Bobby Mackey's is extremely and violently haunted. It's held to be home to over forty reported spirits. The dumping of untold thousands of gallons of blood and other animal parts down the basement well laid the groundwork for the haunting. The grisly disposal of Pearl Bryan's missing head kicked things off, way back in 1896. The basement was the foundation, both figuratively and literally, for the violence that went on upstairs.

Shortly after Bobby purchased the building, his wife Janet

was thrown down the stairs by an entity she felt was Alonzo Walling, the accomplice to Pearl Bryan's murder and decapitation. Janet never went into the building again. Witnesses have been slapped, scratched, growled at, even thrown across the room.

Not all of the manifestations are that aggressive. Johanna's spirit tugs gently on people's clothes with a faint touch. She is always accompanied by the signature scent of her rose perfume. Other reports include sightings of the full body apparitions of both Johanna and Pearl Bryan. Furniture moves by itself. The jukebox turns on and off, and occasionally plays songs that aren't in its repertoire. Bangs and disembodied screams split the air. And deep growls drift up from the old slaughterhouse well.

Bobby himself doesn't believe in any of this. He's content to just make his music and entertain his fans. The paranormal community's interest in his club is largely due to a guy named Carl Lawson.

Bobby hired Carl to work at the club, and as part of his pay, Carl was given the use of an apartment in the building. Living there, in close contact with all the dark spiritual energy swirling around the place, Carl became very familiar with the spirits of Bobby Mackey's Music World. Some say he became a little too familiar with them ...

In 1991, activity in the club reached a fever pitch. Carl had been telling Bobby for months about the encounters he'd been having with the resident spooks. Eventually, Carl began having serious trouble with the supernatural activity swirling around his apartment. He claimed he'd been possessed by the demons of the basement portal. (Carl had actually been the one to discover the well, after dreaming about it while living in the apartment. He would have nightmares about an entity he called "Charlie", in which the spirit would tell him to go down into the basement and dig.) An exorcism was performed, with somewhat limited results. Carl was still tormented by the spirits of the place. Carl Lawson passed away in 2012, and it is said that his ghost, too, has joined the motley crew that haunts Bobby Mackey's Music World.

Interestingly, when he was interviewed by Zak Bagans for

the television show *Ghost Adventures*, Carl told the investigator that he wanted to be buried at the building when he died. This is puzzling—why would someone who suffered so terribly from paranormal activity want to spend eternity at the scene of his troubles? Longtime employee Wanda Kay, who leads paranormal tours at Bobby Mackey's, theorizes that even after Carl's exorcism, the supernatural was a part of him. He lived there, true, and he had close relationships with the spirits of the place. Wanda told *Ghost Adventures* that Carl was always begging to come back into the building. And he's not alone. Matt Coates, Director of Security at Bobby Mackey's, has quit several times, only to come back the very next morning. He says that the atmosphere of the building is constantly changing.

Ghost tours of the building are often led by Gatekeeper Paranormal. The women of Gatekeeper Paranormal take a scientific approach to their work, and are not interested in all the hype about the evil that may or may not lurk in the basement. Still, even they are affected by the mystique that infuses the nightclub.

"The best EVP we got was a female voice saying a long sentence, which is weird because normally its just a word or two," Laura Roland told the website bittersoutherner.com. "But this one is kind of a whisper, and in kind of a Southern accent, and it says, *'she does not like all these people in here'*." Understandable, that a well-bred Southern lady might be uncomfortable in a rough-and-tumble place like the Primrose, or the Latin Quarter, or The Hard Rock Cafe. Even Bobby Mackey's Music World might not be to this fastidious spirit's taste. The four investigators all agree that sometimes the paranormal vibe in the building is so ugly that they won't stay in there alone.

Investigator James Barrow, of Spirits in the Night, visited the building on October 17, 2019. The group launched into the evening by going straight down to the basement to check out the well. Barrow captured an EVP insisting *"get out of the basement"*. On his RT-EVP recorder (a device that spits out voices in "real time"), a woman pleaded *"please help me"*, and a man snarled *"F--- you … in your mind."* A female investigator explained to the spirits how to use a device to communicate, and a timid voice muttered, *"Pearl's here"*. Soon, though, the antagonistic entities returned. Voices spat, *"Get out of this basement"*, *"F--- this building"*, and *"Go f--- with yourself."*

The abuse wasn't just verbal. An investigator got scratched on the back of her neck during her visit. A return, later that evening, to the "portal to Hell" resulted in a very clear EVP of a petulant spirit whining, *"Will you stop recording?"*

Carl Lawson also put in an appearance that evening. Barrow had a conversation with Lawson via a ghost box, a device that turns phonetic sounds into speech. Barrow asked, "Is Carl Lawson here tonight?"

A deep voice replied, *"In the bar room."* Moments later, the same voice inquired, *"Still recording?"* Barrow plunged ahead, saying, "Good to meet you, Carl, my name's James. How're you doing?"

The spirit admitted, *"Good."*

Some of the interactions with the entities in the basement, near the old well, were heartbreaking and very human. At one point, a female investigator asked, "How long have you been here?"

The reply, through the ghost box, was haunting: a plaintive *"We forgot."* Another response to the same question was a thoughtful, *"A long time."* Another spirit said, panicking, *"We're trapped here!"* An investigator asked, "Are we safe down here?" A female spirit snapped back, *"Near the well you're not..."*

The entities in the building are perfectly honest about their situation. Near the end of the evening, an investigator standing near the well asked aloud, "Why is everybody so afraid to be down here? What happened? What's so bad?"

The answer came immediately through the RT-EVP device, a barely discernible growl.

"Demons."

Celia Rose, Teenage Poisoner (1896)

Once upon a time, late in the nineteenth century, there was a girl named Celia Rose, who lived in Pleasant Valley, Ohio. With a pretty name like Celia Rose, living in a place called Pleasant Valley, you might be picturing a dainty girl with porcelain skin and cascades of golden curls, a demure damsel whose greatest joy would be to sit and work on her embroidery.

You would be wrong.

Celia Rose, or Ceely as she was called, was a big, ungainly farm girl, often described as "painfully plain". She lived with her parents, David and Rebecca Rose, and her brother Walter, who was twenty years older than Ceely. Ceely was probably an "oops" baby, as her parents were both past forty, well into middle age when she came along. Rebecca herself often wondered if that's why Ceely seemed simple.

Ceely wasn't what that era considered an imbecile. She was just a bit slow, and had zero ambition. (Her brother Walter wasn't too sharp of a tack, either.) She was an avid reader, although she was slow to pick up both reading and writing. She devoured all the books the family owned, reading them several times. Her father subscribed to several newspapers, and Ceely read them all front to back, saving them to read again later. But she never did anything with that modicum of intelligence. She made her way through school, and that was it. In fact, she was held back so many times that when she finally dropped out of school at the age of fourteen, she was in classes with children half her age. Her father and brother worked the family's grist mill, called the Schrack Mill, and her mother did a lot of canning to keep the family fed. Ceely helped if she felt like it.

Ceely wasn't dainty or even attractive, but people in the neighborhood treated her with kindness when they weren't ignoring her. Nobody really disliked her; she just wasn't popular. As a child, she shunned the company of other children, preferring to build elaborate dollhouses of twigs and flowers on the banks of a stream near her home. She spent hours in her own little world, where she could forget for a while about the other children calling her "ugly old Ceely!". She did have a couple of girl friends from school, sisters named Cora and Theresa (Tracy) Davis.

The Roses were neighbors with the Berry family, but the families weren't close at all. George Berry lived close to the Roses with his wife, two sons, a daughter, and his elderly father. Even though the Berry's front door was just twenty yards away from the Roses' mill, the two families barely spoke. David Rose was known to keep to himself, and resented it when anyone questioned him about his business. Walter inherited these traits, and to a higher degree. Walter had a fiery temper, but he wasn't vindictive. You just didn't cross the Rose men. The Berrys, on the other hand, were prosperous and well-liked. They owned many acres of beautiful, productive farmland. They had the reputation of being generous, warm-hearted folks... they just didn't have anything to do with the Roses.

All that changed in 1896. Since Ceely only did housework when she felt like it, that gave her plenty of time to wander the woods and fields around the house. One fine spring day, Ceely spied Guy Berry plowing in his father's field. The 24-year-old Ceely became infatuated with the good-looking teenager (Guy was 17).

Guy, like everyone else, was polite to Ceely, but he really wasn't interested in a relationship with her. To Ceely, though, Guy's friendly chatter was the next best thing to a marriage proposal. For several months, she met Guy as often as she could, her simple mind awhirl with romantic possibilities. Guy politely endured her visits, which just gave Ceely more fantasy-fodder. She even told Guy during one conversation that they would be married within three years. (This was, of course, completely arbitrary, and news to Guy.) Guy tried to let her down easy, telling her that the reason they couldn't be together was that her parents didn't approve of him (the classic "it's not you, it's me" approach).

Eventually, other Berry family members realized the depth of Ceely's feelings for Guy. Claude, Guy's 12-year-old brother, came right out and told Ceely bluntly that Guy wasn't going to marry her, and that in fact he had a girlfriend. Ceely brushed off the unwelcome news, saying she'd marry Claude instead. He begged off, telling her he was too young to get married.

"I can wait until you grow up," was Ceely's placid response.

This was really too much for the Berrys. Guy went to his father and told him he was tired of Ceely hanging around all the time. George Berry paid a visit to David Rose and asked him to control his daughter. Embarrassed, David came home and yelled at Ceely for disgracing the family. Rebecca and Walter chimed in too. Everyone was sore at Ceely for her indiscretion.

Ceely's mind worked slowly, but it worked. In late June, 1896, Ceely's revenge began. In retaliation for the reprimand, Ceely took arsenic that her brother had bought as rat poison, and filled a pepper box with it. (Some versions of the tale say that she soaked fly paper to get the arsenic off of it, but why bother to do that when you can just pop open a box of Rough on Rats?) On June 30, she sprinkled the arsenic-laced pepper on the cottage cheese her family liked to have for breakfast.

David took a big helping of the cheese, and ate it all. He died of arsenic poisoning the same day. Walter didn't have quite as much. He died a week or so later, on July 5. To avoid any suspicion, Ceely herself took a helping of the cheese too, but only pretended to eat it. Later, she threw it out into the yard. Seven chickens ate the cheese. They all died.

Rebecca began to recover, as she hadn't eaten as much of the poisoned cheese. But as she began to get better, she asked Ceely straight-up if she had been responsible for the deaths of David and Walter. (The doctors had waited for two days to tell Rebecca of the other deaths, as she was so ill herself, but Rebecca had her suspicions. Rebecca herself was asked about the suspicious deaths, and said she had no idea how poison could have gotten into the cheese, as she had fixed the breakfast herself. Only later did she admit that Ceely had helped her prepare breakfast that day.) The local paper had an account of the confrontation; a neighbor woman was in the next room at the time, and overheard the conversation.

"Celia, could you have done such an awful thing?" Rebecca asked one day after she was able to sit up in bed. "God help you if you did."

"Why, Ma," the young woman answered, "what makes you ask me such a question? If you had not said anything about the rat poison nobody would have suspected me at all."

"Look me in the face, child," Rebecca said, "and tell me the truth."

Ceely simply hung her head. That was answer enough.

Then Rebecca dropped a bombshell... she told Ceely they had to move. Ceely was already under suspicion for two deaths, and Rebecca's only thought was to protect her daughter. Ceely was not about to be separated from her crush, so she retrieved the pepper box from under the dock plant in the garden where she'd hidden it, and dosed Rebecca's bowl of bread and milk with more arsenic. Rebecca died early the next morning, on July 20.

Suspicion for the deaths (human and chicken) naturally fell on Ceely, as she was the only family member not taken sick. She hung out at home for a few days, then went to the home of John Ohler and his family, who were friends of the Roses. Ceely quickly wore out her welcome at the Ohlers'. She was just as uninterested in helping around their house as she had been at home. She sighed with exaggerated relief when she was taken to jail, saying "I have been working so hard at Mrs. Ohler's." (Mrs. Ohler, according to the newspaper accounts, said "the extent of her labors was to lie at length on a sofa until the bell rang for meals.")

Augustus Douglass, the prosecuting attorney, wanted to be sure Ceely had committed the crime before he took her to court. He asked Theresa Davis, who had been friends with Ceely when they'd been at school together, to try and worm a confession out of her.

Theresa invited Ceely to sit with her at the Ohlers' and chat, just a bit of girl talk. Well into their conversation, she spun a (totally fictional) tale of forbidden love. She told Ceely that she'd met a handsome young man, with hair the color of sun-kissed wheat and warm, sky-blue eyes. But, Theresa complained, her parents had forbade the relationship. Whatever should she do? she asked.

"Kill 'em, Tracy. Kill 'em all," was Ceely's response. "That's what I did."

Ceely opened up to her former friend, saying at first that Guy had suggested she poison her family so they could run off and get married. The next day, though, she admitted that Guy had nothing to do with the killings.

Ceely also admitted to all three murders, saying that she had indeed sprinkled rat poison on the cottage cheese. When she heard the doctors say that Rebecca was beginning to recover, she snuck over and put more arsenic on the bowl of bread and milk her mother had fixed for herself. She told Theresa that her mother had complained that the milk "tasted funny." Then, when Rebecca started vomiting, her body desperately trying to eject the poison, Ceely laughed at how well the arsenic was working.

Celia was arrested and tried for the three murders. Constable Pluck, Augustus Douglass, and Cora Davis all visited Ceely in jail, wondering what else Ceely would say in front of her school friend. Douglass warned her that anything she said could be used against her in court. Of course, Ceely went ahead and repeated her story of poisoning the cottage cheese; she'd fully intended to kill her family, and she didn't care who knew it. She repeated the story again to several doctors who visited her in jail, the doctors who had treated Walter and Rebecca.

Ceely didn't appear to feel any remorse whatsoever for her crimes. In one of her jailhouse interviews, someone asked her point-blank if she was sorry for what she'd done. Her response was given in a dull monotone as she stared at the floor. "Of course I feel bad and all that. I am all alone." But she seemed to be saying what she felt her questioner wanted to hear.

Ceely was tried three times, each count of murder being a separate court appearance. The trial for the murder of her father, David Rose, began on Monday afternoon, October 12, 1896. When Ceely went to trial, both the prosecution and the defense agreed that the main issue was determining Ceely's responsibility for the crimes. Guilt was secondary; she'd already confessed several times. But had she known what she was doing?

Coroner George W. Baughman testified that Celia told him first that she didn't think that the family's sickness had been caused by anything they'd eaten, but later told him in detail that she'd poisoned them all. George Berry, Guy's father, told the court that he had complained to David Rose about Ceely bothering Guy and Clyde when they were supposed to be working. He said, too, that he had visited the Roses when Walter and Rebecca were sick, and had noticed several dead chickens in the yard.

Ceelys' friend Tracy Davis spoke of attending parties and literary society meetings together, saying she'd known Ceely for about fifteen years. She said that she tried to ask Ceely about her father's death, but that Ceely didn't want to talk about it. Instead, she preferred to fantasize about the wonderful life of wedded bliss that would be hers when she married Guy. Tracy said that she, Cora, and Ceely went to the Roses' barnyard and found the pepper box under the broad leaves of a dock weed, just where Ceely had said she'd thrown it. Ceely picked it up and peered inside it, saying, "Oh, there's some of it right now. I thought I'd washed it all out."

Many people testified to Ceely's simple-mindedness. Lavina Andrews, another schoolmate, said that Ceely did poorly in school, and mostly just seemed interested in watching the boys play ball at recess. Mrs. Ohler claimed that Ceely would never be able to earn a living for herself (although she was skilled at needlework; the Roses' family effects were sold at auction to raise money for Ceely's court costs, and many pieces of her handiwork were sold for a good price). Several of Ceely's teachers, Eva Tucker, Mrs. Willard Darling, and Emma Halderman, agreed that Ceely was weak-minded or "silly"—a nice way of saying mentally deficient. Eva Tucker gave her opinion that Ceely had never been taught right from wrong, and so could not be expected to know the enormity of what she'd done. She, too, believed that Ceely could not make her way in the world on her own without being cared for.

Reverend E. H. Dolbeer was called to testify to Ceely's sanity. He admitted that he was not an expert, but had testified in murder cases before. He stated that Ceely was not a raving maniac, but that she was most definitely insane. "Celia will not do a thing if told not to do it. If Celia had been taught for years that murder was wrong she would have known it was wrong. But she was not of sound mind when I first saw her."

The jury retired for ninety minutes. At the end of their deliberations, Celia Rose was found not guilty by reason of insanity. Augustus Douglass didn't ask for any punishment; instead, Ceely was judged to be a ward of the state and was sent to the Toledo State Asylum. When the Lima State Hospital for the Criminally Insane was completed in 1915, she was transferred there. She died there on March 14, 1934, the day after her 61st birthday.

Ceely's house still stands in what is now Malabar Farms State Park. It's a private residence, but the family allows occasional ghost tours in the house. The house has been featured on *Ghost Hunters*, in the episode "Family Plot". Other investigators have captured evidence at the house.

CAPERS (Carey Area Paranormal Energy Research Society, and isn't that just a great name?) took a tour of the house. The investigators were in a room on the second floor of the small home. One of them asked Ceely, "Is this your bedroom?" A soft female voice replied *"No"*.

Frick and Frack Paranormal also captured an EVP during their September 2019 visit, a voice that said, *"I take it all back."* An investigator asked, "Do you feel bad about what you did?" and got the quiet response, *"I do"*.

On quiet nights, people still sometimes see Celia Rose looking out of the windows by the light of the full moon. Perhaps she's hoping for one more glimpse of Guy, plowing the fields with his shirt off. (The sightings seem to happen more frequently during harvest season, so maybe there's something to that theory.)

It's not only the house that's haunted. The murdered Rose family members, and Guy Berry himself, are all buried in Pleasant Valley Cemetery, just across the road from Malabar Farm. Ceely is said to wander the cemetery, maybe keeping watch over the grave of her beloved. She also haunts the prison cemetery at Lima State Mental Hospital where she is buried. Grave 301, labeled simply "C. Rose", is the only grave with a photograph on it. The picture is of Ceely in her younger years; it was taken in September 1896, when she was being held in Richland County Jail. The picture shows a plain, round-faced girl, her arms crossed, staring into the camera with a truculent tilt to her head. Is Ceely the "Angel in White" that is said to wander the cemetery?

Author Mark Jordan, who wrote both a play about Celia Rose and a book called *The Ceely Rose Murders at Malabar Farm*, visited Ceely's grave while doing research for the play. He reported that the day of his visit was gloomy and overcast, with gray clouds scudding across the leaden sky. As he stood in front of Ceely's grave, he was overcome by the sensation that he should explain himself. Silently, he told Ceely that he simply wanted to tell her story with respect and love. At that moment, he says, the clouds parted and a ray of sunlight illuminated Ceely's grave for about ten seconds—and only her grave. The beam of light didn't shine anywhere else in the cemetery, or on the surrounding landscape.

The barn at Malabar Farms is also haunted. Pulitzer Prize-winning author Louis Bromfield bought the Rose house and the land surrounding it in 1939, and named his new holding Malabar Farms. When Bromfield bought the property, he had David Rose's mill torn down, and beams from the building were repurposed in the construction of a barn. The barn is now home to a theater company which offers an annual production of three ghost story plays, including Mark Jordan's play about Ceely Rose.

Jordan was watching a rehearsal of his play when one of the stage lights, which had never malfunctioned before, started flickering during the scene in which Ceely kills her mother. When the scene was over, the flickering stopped.

Ceely Rose, despite her horrendous deeds, is one of Ohio's favorite spirits. She has been honored by Phoenix Brewing Company in nearby Mansfield, Ohio, with her very own beer: Ceely Rose White IPA. "Our current infatuation with white IPAs can only be compared to the white hot love obsession of Ceely Rose." Describing the beer as wheat-based with fruity hops and notes of orange and coriander, the description archly says, "Trust us, you will prefer our spice combinations to Ceely's..." The brewers seem to have an odd sense of humor anyway— the brewery and taproom are located in the restored Schroer Funeral and Mortuary Home. The brewing equipment and cold storage are housed, appropriately enough, in what used to be the embalming and prep area. And the former chapel is now a beautifully renovated taproom. Other beers on offer include Black Aggie, John Doe, Toe Tag, Tipped Tombstone, Ferryman, and Krampus Kandy. These folks have *fun* with their beers.

Murdered By Poverty (1901)

The children's toys are scattered on the ground and stacked on top of the headstone. A stuffed horse. A furry gorilla. A cloth piggie. A string of gold beads—you can almost see the seeking fingers of a curious toddler reaching for them. A baby doll, its terrycloth onesie gray with age and weather, is propped at the base of the stone. A couple of plastic dinosaurs wait their turn to go into the Fisher Price barn. Toy cars, too many to count at a glance, are placed with gentle care on and around the monument. A Barbie knockoff sits atop the stone, a polite smile pasted on her face, her hair shaggy—its only the wind that combs it these days—her hand up in a cheerful plastic wave to anyone who stops by for a visit. And visitors do stop by; people have been putting offerings of children's toys and trinkets here for years.

This is the stone that marks the mass grave of the six Naramore children. Ethel Marion, age 9, Charles Edward, age 7, Walter Craig, age 5, Chester Irving, age 4, Elizabeth, age 3, and Lena Blanche, 6 months, were killed on March 21, 1901. Most of them were hit in the head with an axe; baby Lena was clubbed to death. These are the facts of their deaths ... but, as always, there is more, much more, to their story, which began in love and ended in bloodshed.

Elizabeth Ann Craig, 19 years old, married Frank Lucius Naramore on October 25, 1890. Their first child, Ethel, was born eight months later. The young family settled in Oakham, Massachusetts. Five more children followed in quick succession, which put a strain on the family finances.

Lizzie, according to neighbors, was a hard worker and a

loving mother, but she couldn't keep the household running all by herself. Frank had a well-paying job at the sawmill of the Parker Lumber Company, but he was not the best provider. He usually drank his paycheck, and ran around with other women while Lizzie waited at home with the kids.

By March 1901, after ten and a half years of marriage and six kids, Lizzie was at her breaking point. She'd reached out to family and friends for help, but it just wasn't enough. Finally, at her wits' end, she contacted a welfare organization called the Overseers of the Poor in Baldwinville, Massachusetts.

A cluster of social workers visited the Naramore house. What they found, at the end of a hard winter, appalled them. There was no heat in the house, and little food. The group made their recommendation: for the safety and wellbeing of the Naramore children, they would be taken from the home. The five oldest would be farmed out to foster homes, and six-month-old Lena would be placed in the poor house in the town of Holden. The social workers promised to return in a week to take care of the situation.

This may have been somewhat of a wake-up call for Frank Naramore. On the morning of March 21, he swung by the grocery store on his way to work, and ordered some flour and other supplies to be delivered to Lizzie at home.

Around 2:45 that afternoon, George Thrasher, the delivery boy, arrived at the Naramore home. As he came closer, he began to get the feeling that something was very wrong. He knew the Naramores had six kids ... but he couldn't hear any of them playing. Six kids, they ought to be making some kind of noise.

George tried the front door, and found it locked. Now concerned, he peered through a bedroom window, and saw a pool of blood spreading under the bed. He shouldered the door open with a splintering smash, realizing that the door had been barricaded with a piece of wood ... from the inside.

Stunned at the amount of blood in the bedrooms, George ran for help. He came back with a couple of men from town. The scene that met them in the Naramore house was horrifying.

The two oldest children, nine-year-old Ethel and seven year old Charles, were laid out on the bed in one bedroom. They had both been killed by axe blows to the head. In another bedroom, also laid out, were five-year-old Walter, four year old Chester, and three year old Elizabeth. All three had also been hit in the head with an axe. Lizzie was on the bed too, her throat slit, drenched in blood just like her dead children. In her arms was six-month-old Lena, who had been beaten to death with a club.

The townspeople were sickened by the scene of slaughter. Who could have committed such an atrocity—the murder of six children and their young mother? Someone reached out to take Lena's battered body from Lizzie's embrace ...

... and Lizzie stirred. There was life in her yet, despite the bloody gash in her throat. She was taken to a nearby hotel. Slowly, a doctor brought her back from the brink of death. Deputy Sheriff Sylvester Bothwell was brought in to talk to her. Perhaps she'd seen her attacker? Maybe she could identify the person who'd murdered every single one of her children?

As it turned out, Lizzie did indeed know who had killed the six Naramore children, and had attacked her.

She herself had done it.

When the social workers from the Overseers of the Poor had left the Naramore home a week before, Lizzie knew she had some hard decisions to make. She knew full well that her children's lives would never be the same if she allowed them to be taken away. It was rare for siblings to be sent to the same foster family; her children would be scattered to the winds. And what kind of life would baby Lena have? Torn from her mother's loving arms at only six months old? No, Lizzie thought, she couldn't let that happen to her darlings. She would take care of her children the best way she could.

She locked the doors of the house, barricading them further with pieces of wood. Then she called her oldest child, Ethel, into the kitchen. Did she hug the girl tightly? Did she smooth Ethel's hair back from her forehead with a tender touch? Did she whisper in the girl's ear—"I love you so much," perhaps? We'll never know.

Then she lifted a double-bladed axe and chopped into Ethel's skull.

When Ethel was dead, Lizzie carried her into her bedroom

and laid her out on the bed. Then she called Charles into the kitchen. Did she say anything to her oldest son? "I'll always love you" … or maybe "I'm sorry"? We'll never know what words passed between Lizzie Naramore and her children as she took their lives, one by one, going down the line according to age.

After killing Charles with the axe, she laid him out next to Ethel. Then she killed Walter, and laid his body gently in another bedroom. Then she killed Chester. And she killed Elizabeth. She used the axe to split their heads open, calling them into the kitchen and dispatching each one, as though methodically dosing them with cod liver oil as a spring tonic. She laid Chester and Elizabeth out next to Walter.

Was baby Lena crying by now, alerted by some weird sense that something in the house was very wrong? Maybe Lizzie picked her up and soothed her, bouncing her a bit as she held the baby close to her heart. Then she put Lena down and clubbed her to death.

Lizzie's work was nearly done. Perhaps she went into the first bedroom once more, to tell Ethel and Charles goodbye. Then she came back into the bedroom where Walter, Chester, and Elizabeth were laid out. She clutched her husband's straight razor, took a deep breath, and slashed her own throat. To make sure of death, she also lifted her skirt and sliced the femoral artery in her inner thigh. Then she let her skirt fall, climbed into bed next to her dead children, took little Lena into her arms for a final cuddle, closed her eyes, and waited to die.

Deputy Sheriff Bothwell listened to Lizzie's confession with mounting horror and grief. He had no choice but to take her into custody as soon as she recovered from her suicide attempt.

Frank Naramore was crazed with grief at the loss of his children. But his remorse came far too late. The funeral was held at Barre Congregational Church, and in preparation, Reverend Charles Talmadge did a little digging into the family's situation. What he discovered appalled him. Talmadge used his funeral sermon to point a finger not only at Frank Naramore for his neglect, but also at society in general for allowing the Naramores to live in such extreme poverty that Lizzie saw only one way out of her dire predicament.

(Chillingly, Lizzie's killing of her children was not the only crime committed on March 21. The very next article in the March 22, 1901 edition of *The Lewiston Daily Sun*, after an article on the Naramore murders, reported that three children had been killed in a nearby town. Jacob Dearborn Marr, a farmer living about eight miles from town, killed his three children—Alice M, age 13, Elwin, age 9, and Helen, age 7—with an axe on March 21, the same day the Naramore children were slaughtered. The family had just gotten up from the dinner table, and Alice was washing dishes at the kitchen sink. Her father went past her to the shed, and came back carrying an axe. He struck Alice in the head—a single blow was enough to kill her. While his wife ran screaming from the house, Jacob went upstairs and killed Elwin and Helen, too. As they sat playing, he attacked. Again, one hit from the axe each was enough to take the children out. Jacob's wife, meanwhile, ran to Jacob's father's house for help. When Samuel Marr came in, Jacob was calmly washing his hands at the sink. Samuel asked Jacob why he had killed his three young children. Jacob simply said, "I don't know." This was his answer to every question put to him that day.)

Lizzie Naramore went to trial for murder. Knowing her situation, the Commonwealth charged her only with the murder of Ethel, her oldest child. Lizzie was found not guilty by reason of insanity. She was placed in the state mental hospital in Worcester to serve a life sentence, but was released five years later, on November 30, 1906, as sane.

The murders of the Naramore children led to a change in child protection policies. In 1903, the Massachusetts Society for Prevention of Cruelty to Children took another look at its policy. The rule had been that "prevention of cruelty to children" meant protecting abused and neglected children by taking them away from their families. With the Naramore tragedy in their sights, though, the Society changed its focus, to work with troubled families to prevent children being removed from the home.

The cemetery in Coldbrook Springs didn't have a paupers section, and even though the community was aghast at what had happened to the Naramore children, no one volunteered to pay for a burial in the churchyard of the Baptist church.

Sylvia Shults

The children were laid to rest outside Riverside Cemetery in nearby Barre, to the left of the cemetery gates. The mass grave was unmarked for over a century, but in 2002, citizens took up a collection to erect a granite tombstone. The stone has the children's names and dates on one side. On the other side is carved the story, in a nutshell, of the terrible choice Elizabeth Naramore made to save her children from grinding poverty and a life of growing up in separate foster homes.

The Naramore children sleep in a clearing carved from the Massachusetts woods. A lightning-blasted tree stands guard over the gravestone. Paranormal author Joni Mayhan has visited the grave. "It's hard to stand there and not feel a rush of emotion," she says.

"The energy hung in the air like a bank of fog, surging around us as if trying to get our attention." Other paranormal investigators have also experienced this restless energy. It's completely subjective, but it's hard not to imagine six young spirits milling about the place where they are buried.

In addition to the many toys left as friendly offerings to the young ghosts, there are also several solar lights on the grave. That way, the children aren't alone in the dark as the sun sets and the long shadows of the trees crowd in at dusk. Really, they aren't alone anyway.

They have each other.

Screaming Lizzie (1905)

Some guys just can't take no for an answer.

Edward Robhaut carried a torch for a pretty young thing named Lizzie Kaussehull. He was constantly sending her flowers, writing her letters professing his love, and generally being a pest. This was in 1905, and the term "stalker" wasn't quite in use in the popular vernacular, but Robhaut was definitely a stalker.

Robhaut was so smitten with Lizzie that he would hang around at the corner of Lincoln and Carmen Avenues in Chicago, waiting for the streetcar that Lizzie took home from her job (she worked at Moeller and Stange's grocery store, farther south on Lincoln Avenue). When Lizzie would get off the streetcar, Robhaut would invariably be there waiting for her. She tried to ignore him as she walked home from the streetcar stop, but that was hard to do with a creeper following her.

And Edward Robhaut took creepiness to the next level. He told Lizzie that if she didn't agree to marry him, he would kill her. (What girl could resist such charm? Feel free to roll your eyes.) Lizzie was genuinely afraid for her life, and rightly so. Her family reported Robhaut's stalkerish behavior to the police. Robhaut was arrested, and placed under a "peace bond" (an old-fashioned name for a restraining order) on November 11. Unfortunately, this did nothing to stop his creepy behavior. He continued to follow Lizzie home from her stop every afternoon, begging her to marry him, and threatening to kill her if she didn't.

The restraining order had zero effect in protecting Lizzie's life. After stalking Lizzie for three months, Robhaut carried out his direst threat. Lizzie still refused to marry him ... so she paid the price.

On November 18, 1905, Lizzie got off the streetcar as usual, surrounded by several of her girlfriends from work. Within the protection of the group, Lizzie was laughing and chatting, her stalker temporarily forgotten.

Then Lizzie saw Robhaut leaning against a nearby wall. She froze, and the chatter of the group died as the girls turned to follow her gaze. Lizzie held up a hand as if to ward off Robhaut's manic stare, and stammered that he still had a peace bond against him.

Things happened very quickly after that. The sight of sweet Lizzie, who had rejected him, sent Robhaut into a high-speed come-apart. Gripping the handle of a knife, he seethed with resentment and rage. Suddenly Robhaut broke away from lounging against the storefront and rushed at Lizzie, who started to shriek. She didn't even have time to plead for her life—all she could do was scream. Her cries of terror were drowned in blood as Robhaut plunged the knife into her chest. She staggered back, but he followed, stabbing her three more times. She fell to the sidewalk, her bodice soaked in scarlet, her life draining away as she hit the ground. Robhaut spared the object of his obsession just one more glance. Then he pulled out a revolver, shoved the stubby barrel into his mouth, and squeezed the trigger, blowing the back of his skull off. His body collapsed on top of Lizzie's; he was dead before he landed.

A murder-suicide, out in the open on a public street, is a surefire recipe for a haunting. Ever since the tragedy, Lizzie Kaussehull has haunted the corner of Lincoln and Carmen. The streetcar Lizzie stepped down from on that fateful day is long gone, but the ghost of the pretty young murder victim remains. On nights when a full moon paints the sky with silver, Lizzie can still be heard. For her shrieking cries that echo into eternity, she has earned a nickname. Locals know her, appropriately, as Screaming Lizzie.

Colonel Pritchard
Gets What's Coming To Him (1909)

When you're in business for yourself, it's good to know what works. For Joseph and William Bott, the answer was pretty clear: booze and billiards.

The brothers were born in Zanesville, Ohio, sons of German immigrants who arrived from Bavaria in 1840. Joseph left school at thirteen and came to Columbus in 1871 to seek his fortune. He found it in the pool halls of the city. After knocking around doing odd jobs for a few years, he found work at a billiards parlor, and soon transformed himself into an expert player.

William, known as Billie, joined his big brother a few years later. The brothers opened their own billiards parlor in downtown Columbus. This first venture was such a success that they were able to expand their enterprise. Their pool hall soon boasted forty tables.

Their patrons weren't expected to go thirsty, either. In 1890, the boys founded Bott Brothers Buffet and Billiards, which incorporated a saloon into the pool establishment. In 1880, along with a partner, they had founded the Bott & Cannon Company, a liquor wholesaler. So they had quite the selection of straight and blended whiskeys to offer their patrons. The brothers spared no expense in outfitting their latest watering hole: outside the saloon was an electric sign that depicted a pool table. As patrons watched, a pool cue came into view and pool balls scattered in bursts of colored lights. The brothers also installed a giant clock on the sidewalk outside the bar. Columbus was entranced, and the business became a roaring success. Customers swarmed the place to enjoy a meal or a drink or two, or to shoot some pool.

One of the regulars at Bott Brothers was Colonel Randolph Pritchard. Pritchard was a great guy, and the other patrons at the bar as well as the employees enjoyed his company—until he'd had a few belts. A few shots of the Bott brothers' high-end whiskey, and Pritchard turned from a congenial companion to a nasty, abusive jerk. Usually, it was women who suffered when the colonel slipped into one of his liquor-fueled foul moods. Pritchard was known to be very fond of women, but he often lashed out at them for no good reason, especially when he was drunk.

On a snowy February night in 1909, Colonel Pritchard was one of the few patrons who braved the cold to come out to the bar. At about 10 pm, Pritchard blew in on a gust of wintry wind. As the door slammed behind him, the colonel started to brush the snow from his jacket.

Suddenly, the door opened again. A woman ran in and, without saying a word, attacked the colonel with a knife. She got in several deep thrusts with the blade, then ran out again. Pritchard stumbled a few steps, then slumped to the floor. He was dead before the snow began to melt from his boots.

The bar patrons, seeing they could do nothing for Pritchard, flung open the door and rushed out to try to catch the killer. Two men noticed a set of women's footprints in the freshly fallen snow—they led from the front door of Bott Brothers down High Street. They followed the footprints, only to return a few minutes later, empty-handed. They reported that the tracks just sort of petered out. The woman, whoever she was and however Colonel Pritchard had offended her, is believed to have frozen to death somewhere in the city the night she killed him. An investigation went nowhere, no suspects were ever named, and the murder weapon was never found.

What was strange, though, was that the big clock outside Bott Brothers had stopped at 10:05, the exact time of the attack. The Botts had the clock repaired—or rather, they had a repairman look at it. He took the clock apart and couldn't find a thing wrong with it. When he put it back together and reinstalled it on the sidewalk, it started working again. It ran for a while, then stopped again at 10:05. This happened several times, flummoxing several clock repairmen. Finally, the Botts gave up and left the clock stopped at 10:05.

Bott Brothers Buffet and Billiards closed in 1919, but it continued as an eating establishment. For a while it was known (naturally) as The Clock Restaurant, and today it exists as the Elevator Brewery & Draught Haus. The restaurant features excellent food, twelve handcrafted brews, two billiard tables from the 1800s, and the ghosts of Colonel Randolph Pritchard and the scorned woman who took him down.

Pritchard's ghost manifests most often as a feeling of being watched, especially for people who are standing near the original Bott Brothers' billiard tables. He sometimes takes the form of a bright ball of light that drifts through the restaurant.

The colonel's killer stays outside the restaurant. On the anniversary of the murder, if there is snow on the ground, a woman's footprints will appear, starting at the front door of the restaurant and continuing down High Street. People have followed the mysterious footprints in the snow, but no one has ever been able to determine who made them.

The Villisca Axe Murders (1912)

Sometimes, the awfulness of a crime can leave a lasting impression on even the most pleasant place. That's what happened in Villisca, Iowa.

Villisca is a sleepy place even today. On June 10, 1912, it was just another small Midwestern town. Josiah Moore, age 43, had squired his wife Sarah, age 39, to the Presbyterian Church that evening. Sarah had coordinated the Children's Day program at the church, and the Moores' four children – Herman (11), Katherine (10), Boyd (7), and Paul (5) – had accompanied their parents. The Stillinger family was also at the program that night, and since they lived out in the country, Katherine invited Ina and Lena Stillinger to spend the night at the Moore house. Lena was twelve, and Ina was eight, so they were friends to ten-year-old Katherine. With three brothers, Katherine relished the chance to spend time with girls close to her own age.

The program ended at 9:30, and the Moores and the Stillinger girls walked home around 9:45 or 10 pm. They went to bed soon after, with Ina and Lena taking the bed in Katherine's downstairs room, and Katherine bunking with her brothers for the night in their bedroom upstairs.

At 7 am the next day, the Moores' neighbor, Mary Peckham, realized that the Moores hadn't come outside yet to do the morning chores. She knocked on the door, but got no answer. She tried to go inside, but the door was locked ... odd for a small Iowa town in 1912. Mary, a good neighbor, let the Moores' chickens out to forage in the yard, then called Ross Moore, Josiah's brother. Ross came over with his key, and unlocked the door. While Mary waited nervously on the porch, Ross went into the too-quiet house.

Nothing could have prepared him for what waited for him inside. The windows were covered, and Ross walked cautiously through the day-dark of the parlor. He opened the door to the guest room, and recoiled in alarm. Two still bodies lay on the bed, covered with a sheet. There was blood everywhere. Lena had cuts on her arm, and was lying crossways on the bed. Her face had been bludgeoned. Ina was just dead, her face another smashed-in horror.

Ross backed away from the sight, then realized that the deathly silence of the house hadn't changed. He called Josiah's store and got ahold of Ed Selley, an employee. He told Selley to fetch Deputy Marshall Hank Horton, because "something terrible had happened."

Horton arrived at around 8:30, and went into the house. He went up the narrow staircase to the second floor, the wooden steps creaking loudly under his weight.

At the top of the stairs, another horrifying scene awaited him. Josiah and Sarah lay in their bed, their heads covered with sheets, each of their faces pulped by twenty to thirty blows from an axe. The fury of the killer was evident in the gouges left in the room's low ceiling: the murderer was so jacked up with his killing that he hit the ceiling with each backswing of the axe. Horton gulped, and continued on to the children's room.

Blood soaked the bedsheets, the pillows, and the pajamas of the four Moore children. They had also been murdered in their beds; their faces, too, had been obliterated with the blunt side of an axe. Horton came out of the house, stunned at the destruction. He told Ross that he'd found "somebody murdered in every bed."

The theory is this: someone snuck into the Moores' home, possibly while they were at the church. This person hid in the attic, and waited until everyone had gone to bed. (Two cigarette butts found in the attic lent strength to this theory.) Then, when all was still, whoever it was crept out of the attic ... and the slaughter began.

Josiah got the brunt of the killer's fury. The murderer rained more blows on Josiah than on any other victim – and he used the blade on Josiah's face. Every other victim was bludgeoned with the blunt side of the axe head. And the killer really seemed to want to destroy Josiah: his face was so badly damaged that his eyes were missing.

Doctors surmised that the killer attacked the family between midnight and 5 am. The murderer started with Josiah and Sarah, then went into the Moore children's bedroom to slaughter Herman, Mary Katherine, Arthur, and Paul. When the children were dead, the killer revisited the parents, punishing the bodies with yet more blows from the axe, and stumbling over a shoe that had filled with blood, knocking it over into a spreading puddle of gore.

When his murderous work upstairs was finished, the killer went downstairs. In the kitchen, he fixed himself a plate of food, and washed the blood from his hands in a basin of water. Then a noise from the downstairs bedroom caught his attention. He went into the bedroom, grabbing the axe as he went. There he found Lena and Ina Stillinger. They were not spared; their faces were also bludgeoned with the blunt side of the axe blade. Mercifully, investigators theorized that the only person awake for the attacks was 12-year-old Lena, as her arms were up in what may have been a futile attempt to protect her face from the blows. The rest of the victims never knew what happened.

There were several bizarre touches at the crime scene. After the murders, the killer went through the house and ransacked the dresser drawers, using clothing to cover every mirror in the house and the glass windows in the front and back doors. Also, the killer left the axe leaning against a wall ... and next to that was a four-pound slab of bacon, just leaning on the wall next to the axe.

The funerals were held a few days later, on June 12, 1912, in the town square. The Moore family was well-respected in Villisca, and the community was gutted by the multiple murders. The streets were blocked off as a funeral procession fifty carriages long made its way to the town square. After the service, the caskets were taken on several wagons to Villisca Cemetery for burial.

Some kind souls used the funeral as an opportunity to

perform one final service for the family; the bulk of the crime-scene cleanup was done while the funerals were going on. Two men took it upon themselves to get rid of the bloody messes in the bedrooms. One of the men couldn't do it; he had to leave. But the other guy soldiered on. Apparently, he couldn't save the mattresses. He could only roll up the red, sodden masses, tie them with heavy twine, and throw them out the window to land with a horrid thud on the lawn.

Then the investigation began. People had been traipsing through the crime scene for days, so much of the evidence was either destroyed or completely worthless. Tom Churchill, a photographer, was hired by investigators to take pictures of the house before it was cleaned. (Before it was cleaned, but after the victims were taken away: historians have never heard of any existing photographs taken of Josiah and Sarah or of any of the children at the crime scene.) Churchill sold his studio in 1913 to a Mr. Anderson, who sold it to John Warren Noel in 1914. In October 1914, James Wilkerson, a detective from Kansas City, came to the studio and asked Noel if he could see photographs relating to the murder. The photos Noel showed Wilkerson were pictures taken June 11, 1912. They showed the house, bloody bedclothes, and bloodhounds crossing a bridge on the scent of a suspect. But there were no photographs of the bodies.

But these were not the only photographs taken that day. Bruce Stillians, the son of a local druggist, was one of the many people who tromped through the house before the police took control of the crowds. Stillians was a stringer for the *Omaha World* Herald newspaper, so when he went to gawk, he took a small Kodak box camera with him. He managed to snap some shots of the bodies as they lay in the gore-soaked sheets.

Stillians was just doing a job. Maybe he tried to be discreet about it, maybe he didn't – but someone noticed, and took offense. Ross Moore, brother of the murdered Josiah, saw the camera and called Stillians out. His grief fresh and raw, Moore tussled with Stillians for the camera. He easily overpowered the smaller man, and moments later, he hurled the camera to the ground. The camera shattered, the celluloid unspooled ... and the photos were lost forever.

Families in Villisca lived in fear for many weeks, as authorities searched in vain for the killer. Fathers sat up with shotguns, ready to protect their loved ones from attack. But even the most devoted family man must sleep sometimes. Neighbors banded together, cooperating in their vigils. One man of several families stood watch, while everyone else got some much-needed rest, and the men traded off each night.

Witnesses came forward with several suspects. Villisca was a small town, and fingers were pointing every which way. The grosser and gnarlier a crime is, the more weirdos it attracts – people who gravitate to the gruesome, who want to get up close and personal with the icky details. And the weirdos came out of the woodwork for the Villisca murders.

There was no shortage of suspects for the awful crime. Sam Moyer, Josiah Moore's brother-in-law, had often threatened to kill him. He ended up having an alibi. Henry Lee Moore (no relation) was convicted several months after the Villisca murders for the murders of his mother and grandmother. The murder weapon? An axe. (Henry Lee Moore may be responsible for as many as twenty-three axe murders across the Midwest. It's interesting to note that these unsolved murders began in late April 1911 and stopped in mid-December 1912, a window of time when Moore was out of prison.)

Andrew Sawyer was a vagrant who happened to be in Villisca that fateful Sunday night. There's really no evidence that points to him as any sort of serious suspect; he was just a garden-variety drifter who acted weird. Sawyer made his living as an itinerant laborer, traveling around doing odd jobs. He approached Thomas Dyer, a bridge foreman, on Monday June 11, the day the murders were discovered, and asked about a job. He was wearing a suit, which was fine ... but his pants were soaked up to the knees and his shoes were caked with mud. Not only was this strange, it seemed a bit suspicious to Dyer. Dyer's son would later testify that Sawyer told him that he would show him where the murderer had stepped into a creek, and he showed the younger Dyer some footprints in the marshy ground near the railroad tracks. Why Sawyer would point this out is unclear, as his shoes were also muddy. Dyer and his crew were also freaked out by the fact that Sawyer slept in his clothes ... with his axe next to him. Dyer, overcome by suspicion, finally turned Sawyer in to the police. But Sawyer, as it turned out, had an alibi. The sheriff in Osceola, Iowa, had arrested Sawyer there for vagrancy the night of the murders. At 11 pm that night, Sawyer was unceremoniously hustled aboard a train and told to leave town.

Iowa Senator Frank F. Jones was a former employer of Josiah Moore. Moore had worked at Jones' farming equipment company before leaving to start his own business – taking a lucrative John Deere contract with him. It was no secret that there was bad blood between the two men. Witnesses said that they saw Jones' son Albert talking with Josiah Moore a few hours before the murders. Other witnesses said that saw Albert with W.B. McCaull, who owned a pool hall in Villisca. Even more witnesses said later that McCaull showed them a piece of bone that he claimed was part of Josiah's skull. Yet another witness fingered a couple of men she saw walking past the Moore house about 3 pm the afternoon before the murders. One of them, she said, looked like William "Blackie" Mansfield, a reported "cocaine fiend" who had supposedly deserted from the army.

This confluence of sightings led to a supposition that the four men were working together. Going on this theory, James Wilkerson, the Kansas City detective, began to work the case. In 1916, he announced that he'd solved the Villisca murders. He stated that Senator Jones had hired Blackie Mansfield to kill Josiah Moore for hurting his business. Alice Willard, a nosy Villisca resident, was supposedly the key to breaking the case wide open. She testified that on the night of the murders, she and two other women had driven home from Lincoln, Nebraska, and their car had broken down near the Moore house. Willard said that she saw five men standing in the Moores' yard talking in hushed, secretive voices. She couldn't catch all that they said, but she fortuitously picked out some key words: "Sunday", "after church", "money", and "get Joe first, the rest will be easy." She said that one of the men was Senator Jones.

The case against the men fell apart when Mansfield's

employer produced records that proved that Mansfield had been in Illinois at the time of the murders. Wilkerson was left with egg on his face, and both Senator Jones and Blackie Mansfield sued him for slander. Mansfield won his case against Wilkerson and the Burns Detective Agency, and collected $2,250. Senator Jones didn't do as well. He lost his $60,000 suit, and his career was ruined by the allegations.

And then there is the Reverend Lyn George Jacklin Kelly. This guy was a bona fide weirdo, to say the least. His father and grandfather had also been Methodist ministers in England, so Kelly went into the family business, so to speak. He emigrated to America with his wife in 1904, and served in several parishes across North Dakota, Minnesota, Kansas, Oklahoma, and Iowa between 1904 and 1912. What his flock probably didn't know is that the good reverend had suffered a mental breakdown in his teens, attributed by his mother to excessive study, and it still affected his mind. In 1912, Kelly gave up on the Methodist church, saying "You can starve working for the Methodists," and enrolled in the Presbyterian seminary in Omaha, Nebraska. Scheduled to begin his classes in September 1912, Kelly spent the summer working as a visiting minister, traveling between three small communities in Iowa. Two of these, Pilot Grove and Arlington, were northwest of Villisca, which brought him close to town. He collected a steady series of complaints about his odd behavior, but apparently nothing was severe enough to catch the attention of higher-ups in the church.

That changed in June of 1912. Reverend Kelly arrived in Villisca on the morning of June 9, and actually attended the Children's Day celebration at the Presbyterian Church in which the Moore and Stillinger children performed. At 5:19 the next morning, he left town aboard the westbound number 5 train. While on board, he struck up a conversation with some fellow travelers, telling them that eight people in Villisca had been murdered in their beds as they slept. This could have just been the minister passing on some tragic news ... were it not for the fact that the murders weren't discovered until several hours later.

Two weeks later, Reverend Kelly came back to Villisca. He

stayed with Reverend Ewing, and talked the other minister into taking him to see the house where blood had been shed so liberally. He insinuated himself into a group of investigators by telling them he was a detective, and got himself a tour of the murder house. Kelly became obsessed with the murders. He sent weird, rambling letters about the case to police and investigators, and, creepily, to family members of the deceased, who alerted the authorities.

Reverend Kelly was obviously quite mentally ill. When they got these incoherent, disjointed letters about the murders, the authorities theorized that he could have been making it all up, in some sick bid for attention. A private investigator wrote to Kelly on his own initiative, inviting him to share more details.

Kelly did.

Some of the letters were obviously products of Kelly's fevered imagination, but the authorities kept an eye on him anyway. They didn't find enough on him to justify an arrest, but what he had to say raised a few eyebrows – he spoke of walking past the house and hearing the thud of an axe, and he claimed that Sarah Moore had "reared up in bed" before the killer struck. The police decided to keep quiet tabs on him, just in case.

In 1914, Reverend Kelly showed up in Winner, South Dakota. He had dropped out of the seminary because of money troubles, but he was just down, not out. He placed an ad in the Omaha World Herald for a private secretary. A young woman named Jessamine Hodgson answered the ad, and was shocked at Kelly's response: he said she would do just fine, but that she would have to type in the nude. (This was nothing new; Kelly asked young women to pose nude for him on at least three occasions.) Completely grossed out by this, she took the letter to her pastor, who turned it over to the police. They went to the postal authorities with it, and after fishing a bit with more letters purportedly from Miss Hodgson – which Kelly answered with more and more sleaze – the authorities arrested Kelly for sending obscene material through the mail.

Kelly was convicted in May 1914 for this little stunt, and sentenced to Leavenworth Federal Penitentiary, but he transferred to St. Elizabeth's, a mental hospital. During his therapy there, he wrote to the Attorney General expressing his concern that he might be tried for the murders in Villisca.

By this time, the authorities in Iowa had decided to do something about "that crazy preacher in Nebraska" that kept popping up on their radar. During April of 1917 they put together a case against Kelly, and on April 30, they issued a bench warrant for his arrest. On Monday, May 14, Kelly arrived in Red Oak, Iowa, on the number 5 train – the same train he'd taken out of Villisca nearly five years before. He showed up at the office of Montgomery County Sheriff Bob Dunn that afternoon and turned himself in.

Reverend Kelly was indicted for the murder of Lena Stillinger. Given his propensity for requesting girls to pose for him, and the fact that Lena had been found with her underpants removed and thrown under the bed and her nightgown rucked up around her hips, the prosecution theorized that Kelly had covered the windows and mirrors in the house so that he could gaze at Lena's body at his leisure.

Kelly spent the summer of 1917 in jail awaiting trial. On August 30, police began a marathon interrogation session designed to break Kelly. Kelly was a little guy, only 5'2", and the physically larger cops loomed over him intimidatingly. They took periodic breaks to return Kelly to his cell to think things over. In his cell were two more criminals, who urged him to confess; they knew from experience that this would make things easier on him. (In reality, these "criminals" were plants. One was a deputy sheriff and the other was a newspaper editor.) On the morning of August 31, after a grueling night of having questions fired at him, Kelly dictated a confession, which he signed. He stated that he'd seen a shadow figure who handed him an axe and told him to "slay, slay utterly". He said that he'd been walking past the Moore house and had seen the Stillinger girls getting ready for bed. He heard the Lord's voice say, "Suffer the little children to come unto Me." Kelly said that he fell into a trance-like state, picked up an axe he found on the property, and killed everyone in the house. (He later recanted this confession at his trial.) The first jury deadlocked at eleven to one for acquittal. A second jury acquitted him entirely in November 1917. Reverend Kelly was the only suspect ever tried for the murders. (For what it's worth, the people of Villisca were split about equally in their suspicions. Some of them thought Kelly did the deed, some thought it was Senator Jones.)

A serious theory about the Villisca murders involves the fact that the railroad runs right past the town. This would give the killer easy access to town, and an equally easy getaway. In their 2017 book *The Man From The Train*, authors Bill James and Rachel McCarthy James tell the story of Paul Mueller. Mueller was the only suspect in the 1897 murder of a family in West Brookfield, Massachusetts, for whom he'd worked as a farm hand. The authors believe that Mueller left a trail of destruction behind him as he traveled across the country. They have found dozens of newspaper accounts of whole families murdered in similar circumstances to the Villisca case. In fact, they blame Mueller for at least fifty-nine murders in fourteen separate incidents. The facts in each murder are telling: each family lived near train tracks; the killer struck from a hiding place around midnight when his victims were sleeping and at their most vulnerable; the murderer used the blunt side of an axe rather than the blade, bludgeoning the victims in the head and face; the killer left the axe at the crime scene in plain sight; he covered the victims with blankets, and covered the windows and locked the doors before leaving the house. All of these are consistent with the Villisca murders. Can we lay more than just the Massachusetts crime at Mueller's door?

With its history of violent death, the Villisca Axe Murder house has become a bucket-list destination for many paranormal investigators. The people that visit the house are aware of the dark deeds that stain the house's history. Some claim, too, to be in touch with whatever malevolent energy drove the killer and sang in his heart as he waited for the Moores to get home from church. This potent energy proved to be too much for one investigator to handle.

With such a reputation for gore and mystery, the house is an obvious destination for those interested in either true crime or the paranormal. The home became a museum in the 1990s, and soon got a reputation for being haunted. Museum guests felt a sense of unease in the small house and reported hearing footsteps in empty rooms. The museum's owners, Darwin and Martha Linn, expanded the museum's offerings to include overnight accommodation for paranormal investigators.

Robert Laursen Jr, of Rhinelander, Wisconsin, planned a visit to the Villisca house on November 7, 2014, with his mother and stepfather. Conscious of his personal safety, he brought with him a hunting knife, which he carried in a sheath strapped to his leg.

Johnny Houser, the caretaker of the home, checked the three of them in for their visit. Laursen told Houser that he was going to give the house a piece of his mind – that he planned to provoke whatever dark energy still lingered in the home. Houser brushed it off; he'd heard plenty of big talk in his time as caretaker of the Villisca Axe Murder House.

The next morning, Houser woke up to a nightmare. His social media accounts were blowing up, and dozens of his friends had tagged him. Headlines blared: "Man Stabs Himself at the Murder House."

Deep into the investigation, Laursen was alone in the first-floor bedroom, where the Stillinger girls were murdered. No one knows exactly what happened in the wee hours of the morning, but for some reason, Laursen stabbed himself in the chest. He was rushed to Clarinda Regional Hospital, then taken by medical helicopter to Creighton University Medical Center. He died a couple of times on the helicopter ride, but was resuscitated.

Details emerged later. Laursen had been in the house by himself. Around 12:45 am, his parents heard a scream, and came inside to check on him. (It's interesting to note that the original murders happened around 12:45 am.) They found him lying on the floor with his hunting knife shoved into his chest.

Houser was asked by the owner to go in and clean up after the stabbing. Houser has been in the house countless times, but this time, he was spooked. He made two friends come with him for moral support as he did the job. "I don't know what happened in that house, but I don't want to be alone in that house right now," was his sensible attitude. He described his first hesitant steps into the house.

"There was a bunch of bedding there, all rolled up and covered in blood, and there was a teddy bear foot sticking out of it, covered in blood. I just froze, and I was like 'Not again – not again in this place,' because at that point we didn't know if he was going to live or not," Houser told me.

Astonishingly, Laursen did survive his ordeal. He was later invited to return to the house for a filming of the TV show *Kindred Spirits*. Houser saw Laursen, and finally had the chance to ask the questions that had been burning in his mind since the morning of November 8.

He asked why Laursen had brought a knife to the house. That one was easy. Laursen usually concealed-carried a handgun, but he wasn't familiar with Iowa gun laws. So he erred on the side of caution and chose a knife for protection, rather than his customary gun.

Then came the harder question: what happened that night, in the bedroom, in the dark?

Laursen broke down in tears. He didn't remember.

He'd been alone in the bedroom. He'd been provoking. He'd basically dared the spirits to come at him. Then ... he woke up in the emergency room.

Laursen told Houser that the experience had ruined his life. The public thought he was after money, or wanted to be on TV, or was just plain crazy. Meanwhile, he'd lost all credibility with the paranormal community.

Houser and Laursen walked into the house together, and Houser got another shocking surprise. His voice shaking, Laursen looked up at the ceiling, and apologized to the house and its spectral inhabitants. He said he was sorry for getting loud and for screaming and being so belligerent.

Houser admits that after the 2014 incident, he has never again spent the night alone in the house. He dismisses the idea of an actual supernatural attack – "come on, let's get real," he snorts. But he will say that perhaps there is some energy in the house that preys on people who are unprepared for the emotions that can sweep through them, or who are mentally ill, or otherwise susceptible to extremely dark energies.

He pointed out that Reverend Kelly spoke of a shadow figure who handed him an axe and told him to "slay, slay utterly." Kelly spoke of feeling like he was in a trance, that something else was controlling his actions. In the 1930s, a young couple living in the house experienced paranormal activity. The wife began hearing unexplainable sounds in the house. One night, she woke to see the shadowy figure of an axe-wielding man standing at the foot of her bed. And eerily, Laursen's stabbing was not the only modern violence done in that house.

In the 1960s, a family (mother, father, and two young girls) lived in the house. The girls would wake in terror when they heard the sound of children moaning and crying. Soon, they were also finding their clothes strewn around the room – covering the windows and mirrors. They told their parents about the strangeness, but were ignored. Then something happened that got everyone's attention.

The girls were in the parlor, which opens onto the kitchen, and their father was sitting at the kitchen table. The father, who had always pooh-poohed the idea of ghosts, was sharpening his pocketknife. Suddenly, as if in a trance, he lifted the knife and plunged it through the middle of his hand. The sharp pain snapped him out of his fugue state. He grabbed a towel and wrapped it around his hand to staunch the bleeding. Then he gathered his family and they left the house that night.

The family never returned.

The two girls were coaxed back to Villisca many years later for the filming of a ghost hunting show. Houser was there, and heard them talking in low tones before filming began. Unnoticed, he sidled up to them to eavesdrop ... were they getting their stories straight before going in front of the cameras? Actually, it was nothing like that. The two women were trying – and failing – to bolster each other's courage. Neither of them wanted to set foot in the house again, even though decades had gone by since the incident. "They were the real deal," Houser is convinced.

Johnny Houser is the one who discovered a connection between the Villisca house and the fabulously haunted Malvern

Manor in Malvern, Iowa, about half an hour away. Houser says that he would get phone calls from friends at Malvern – "Hey, your name came up on the Geoport [an investigative tool that uses paranormal energy to produce words]. Honestly, I ignored it the first three or four times it happened. But they kept messaging me." The spirits at Malvern kept calling out Johnny's name. Then, things got even stranger: equipment at Villisca would spit out names like "Inez" and "The Captain", spirits that inhabit Malvern Manor.

If there is a connection (and I see no reason why there shouldn't be), it's almost absurdly simple. Malvern Manor used to be the Cottage Hotel. Built in the 1880s, it provided quality accommodations to train travelers for decades. Malvern and Villisca are two towns along the railway, quite close to each other. And the Cottage Hotel was very much a going concern in 1912. It's not much of a stretch at all to theorize that the killer who struck in Villisca got onto the train there and got off for a while at Malvern, perhaps even spending a night or two at the Cottage Hotel.

There is also a more tenuous connection between the Villisca house and the infamous Sallie House in Atchison, Kansas, to the south. I asked Johnny to explain it to me. There are, as it turns out, several eerie coincidences linking the two properties, something not as easily explained as a hotel convenient to the railroad tracks. The houses have the same address: 508 Second Street. One of the drawings of "Sallie" is the spitting image of a photograph of Katherine Moore, even down to the bow in her hair.

The most telling of the coincidences is this: Debra and Tony Pickman, who lived in the Sallie House and were terrorized by the dark entity there, came to the Villisca house for an overnight investigation. Tony stated that he felt the same dark energy at Villisca that he was all-too-familiar with from his experiences in his former home. During the investigation, Tony began gagging and coughing in the parlor. He retched until he threw up ... and a chunk of bacon landed on the floor. Oddly enough, this happened right where the mysterious slab of bacon was found on the morning of the murders. I have no explanation for this. Neither does anyone else.

I spent the first forty-five minutes of my first visit to the Villisca Axe Murder House exploring the house alone. It was a privilege I'll never forget. I was narrating my experiences into a recorder as I walked through the home, planning to use them for an episode of my true ghost story podcast, Lights Out. (I did produce that episode, and you can find it on YouTube and wherever you listen to podcasts. It's Lights Out #80: Villisca Axe Murder House.)

All was fine until I went into the attic. You'll recall that the murderer spent quite some time in the attic waiting for his victims to be deep in slumber. It was still daylight out, and light poured in through the attic window. It would, I thought, have been a lovely place for children to play on a rainy day. Then I glanced upward. The points of the roofing nails holding the shingles on stuck through the wood of the ceiling. I said aloud, "Wow, if someone was hiding in here waiting to come out and murder people, he'd have to watch his head. You could really hurt yourself if you opened your scalp on these nail points." As soon as the words left my mouth, I was overcome by a panicky feeling that washed over my mind. I "noped" out of the attic and down the stairs like my butt was on fire – I couldn't spend one more moment in that room for the time being. I went back later, of course, with other investigators, but all of a sudden the energy in that room was overwhelming. And it happened just when I mentioned someone getting hurt.

I had one of the strangest experiences of my ghost hunting career at the Villisca House. I was sitting alone in the children's room, not recording, not filming, simply letting the evening unfold around me. I was facing the door, sitting on one of the beds. Suddenly, to my right, I heard a sharp crack in the air over another bed, as though someone had snapped a dry branch about the size of my finger. There have been two times in my career that I have nearly jumped out of my skin from being startled on an investigation. That was one of them.

I don't claim any sensitivity to spirits. I have moments where I feel that a room is paranormally "alive", and I can sense when the energy is low, but I can't see or hear spirits. But there's something special about the Villisca House.

Johnny Houser shared his observations of the house with me, and they jibed with what I have experienced too. He was in the house on June 10, the anniversary of the murders, for an overnight investigation. He said that the energy in the house was just creepily off the charts at one point, and he couldn't get out of the house fast enough. He went outside to collect himself for fifteen minutes or so, then went back in, to find that the energy was perfectly calm. "I was like, what on earth was I so scared of twenty minutes ago? Whatever it was, it's gone now."

The first time I investigated there, I was in the house alone for the first 45 minutes. I was also alone there the next morning. The energy of the house was markedly different at those two times.

When I first entered the house, I had no idea what to expect. I was in a house where eight heinous murders had happened; what lasting effect might that have? But as I explored, I realized that the energy was tranquil. You could feel that this was a home filled with love, where four children were being raised. I spent the night there, and slept peacefully.

But the energy in the house the next morning was very different. I did a final walkthrough, and went upstairs to get one more picture in the room where the Moore children were murdered. It was broad daylight, and there was nothing remotely spooky going on at the time ... but something had changed. I have a really good imagination, and as I was leaving the boys' room to head downstairs, my traitorous mind fed me the mental image of blood-soaked corpses. I thought to myself, the first responders would have carried the children out in their arms, but it would have been more problematic getting the bodies of two adults down the stairs. The authorities, or coroner, or someone, would have had to fireman-carry both Josiah and Sarah down those narrow stairs. The mental image squicked me out so much that I had to fight to walk down the stairs without breaking into a run. The house was filled with nervous, almost frightened vibes. I was no longer comfortable being there alone.

I can't explain this, but I have a theory. I think the two feelings reflect the residual energy in the house at those two times of day. In the evening, I could feel the peace and comfort of a tidy home filled with love. In the evening, the Moores had just come home from church. They were together, with friends visiting, on a beautiful summer evening. It was a peaceful time. And in the morning – well, that's when Ross Moore discovered the family and the Stillinger girls murdered. I think the house remembers that.

The Vampire of Düsseldorf (1913-1930)

What does a serial killer look like?

The police in Düsseldorf, Germany, had had a busy week. It was February 13, 1929, and they were cordoning off a crime scene. The night before, Rudolf Scheer, a 45-year-old mechanic, had stumbled home from a night of boozing it up at a beer hall. On his way home, he'd had the bad luck to run into a knife-happy murderer. The blade had flashed down over and over again in a frenzy of destruction.

The police were already on high alert. Four days earlier, on February 8, 8-year-old Rosa Ohliger had been horrifically slaughtered. The girl had been stabbed a dozen times with a pair of scissors. Then, in an attempt to destroy the evidence, the murderer had doused little Rosa with kerosene and struck a match. The flames had fizzled out without doing too much damage, and the killer had stashed the child's barely burned corpse behind a hedge.

As the police secured the crime scene, they noticed a dapper gentleman watching them from the sidewalk. He asked a few questions, looking on with interest as the detectives worked the scene. The investigators gave the man a sharp look, but he was so well-dressed and so soft-spoken that they soon dismissed him as a possible suspect. They all knew that sometimes, killers revisited the scenes of their crimes. But this looky-loo—he said he'd heard about the murder over the telephone—couldn't possibly be the murderer. With his dapper clothes and his soft, gentle voice, this man was about as far from a typical violent killer as you could get. No, the detectives decided, this podgy, middle-aged fellow with the wispy mustache was just some professional businessman, a banker or maybe an accountant, who'd seen the commotion and swung by for a look to satisfy a twinge of morbid curiosity.

But the investigators were wrong—dead wrong. Peter Kürten, the well-groomed fellow at the edge of the crowd, had a streak of pure evil running through him. He had killed Rudolph Scheer. He had killed Rosa Ohliger. And with those two murders, he'd brought his body count up to four, and possibly six. And that was just the humans.

And Peter Kürten was just getting started.

Kürten was born on May 26, 1883, the oldest of thirteen children, in a suburb of Cologne, Germany. His family was crammed into a one-room apartment, beaten down by extreme poverty, and brutalized by Kürten's father, a sadistic, abusive alcoholic. At nine years old, Peter, who'd been steeped in daily sexual and physical violence all his life, developed an unhealthy relationship with a dogcatcher who lived in the same building. This neighbor introduced the young Peter to bestiality with dogs.

Peter, still only nine years old, also added murder to his resume. He later claimed that he'd drowned two classmates. The three boys were on a rafting trip on the Rhine River, and Peter pushed one of them overboard. The other jumped in to rescue the first one, and Peter held both of them under the raft until bubbles stopped drifting to the surface. At the time, everyone thought it was just a tragic childhood accident, and Peter did nothing to disabuse people of this notion. But the two drowned boys may have been Kürten's first victims.

Peter didn't slow down his sexual experimentation as he grew into his teens. He discovered that sheep, goats, and other farmyard animals were just as much to his perverted tastes as dogs were. The teenager also found out that his pleasure increased when, during intercourse, he stabbed the animal. A farmer caught him *in flagrante delicto* and put a stop to the barnyard antics.

In 1899, Peter turned sixteen, stole what little money there was in the apartment, and ran away from home to escape the daily violence. He left at an opportune moment—just after he ran away, his father was arrested for having incestuous relations with Peter's 13-year-old sister, and spent three years in jail.

Finding himself on the streets, Kürten turned to petty crime, which led to many short stretches in prison. These prison stays exacerbated his sadistic tendencies, and he turned his depravity away from animals and focused it on humans ... and on himself. He discovered a fascination for savage sexual acts while in solitary confinement. Kürten began to break prison rules on purpose, in order to spend as much time in solitary as he could manage.

Kürten was a brutal psychopath, but he knew the value of blending into society. When he was released from prison in 1913, his first stop was at a tailor's shop, where he stole a double-breasted pinstripe suit and a fedora. He knew that camouflage would be the secret to his successful reign of terror.

When he wasn't in prison, Kürten filled his time with sexual assaults. This led inexorably to murder. His first documented murder victim was Christine Klein. Klein, 9 years old, was sexually assaulted in her bedroom at her family's home on May 25, 1913. Kürten had broken into an inn in the town of Köln-Mülheim (a suburb of Cologne) to rob it, and made his way upstairs. He found Christine asleep. He strangled her for about a minute and a half. "The child woke up and struggled but lost consciousness," Kürten later said about this first murder. "I had a small but sharp pocketknife with me and I held the child's head and cut her throat ... the whole thing lasted about three minutes." During the rape and murder, Christine's parents were working in their pub, directly below her bedroom.

Christine's uncle had recently had an argument with her father, so suspicion for the little girl's murder initially fell on him. Kürten returned to the scene of the crime the next day, and was fascinated by the pervasive sense of horror in the neighborhood. The sexual assault only heightened the residents' fear, and Kürten gloried in it. He followed the uncle's trial with keen interest. It didn't matter to him, in the end, that the uncle was found innocent of the murder due to lack of evidence. Kürten had discovered new depths of eliciting suffering in his fellow humans.

Kürten made several visits to Christine's grave over the next few weeks. Getting away with the child's murder heightened his sick confidence. Two months later, he strangled 17-year-old Gertrud Franklin in Düsseldorf. Incredibly, he wasn't caught for this murder either. On July 14, he did go to prison again, though. He'd been called up for military service at the beginning of World War I, but deserted and was caught. He also had a string of burglaries and arsons on his record, so he was imprisoned for his longest stretch to date. This filled him with even more dark, simmering rage.

In April 1921, Kürten was freed again. He moved to Altenburg, where he met and married Auguste Scharf, a former prostitute. Scharf had recently gotten out of jail herself; she'd been convicted of murdering her fiancé. Kürten spent the next four years actually keeping his nose clean.

But it didn't last. In 1925, the Kürtens moved back to Düsseldorf. The area seemed to have some strange pull on Kürten, because he soon returned to his life of crime. He took up petty crime and arson again, and soon the lure of violence was too much to resist. He spent six months in prison for seducing and threatening a servant girl.

And she was one of the lucky ones. Kürten tried four times to strangle women, without success. He went back to stabbing as his preferred method of killing, realizing that he'd found his niche. One victim, an elderly woman named Appollonia Kuhn, actually survived being stabbed repeatedly with a sharpened pair of scissors. She ended up with 24 individual wounds, but lived.

Others weren't so lucky. Rosa Ohliger was stabbed thirteen times by Kürten, who climaxed during the attack, before he tried to burn her corpse. Failing in that, he dumped it behind a hedge. Rosa was just the first victim of Kürten's fifteen-month long crime spree. On August 11, 1929, Kürten picked up a young woman named Maria Hahn, whom he'd met three days earlier. They spent several hours together—then he took her to a nearby meadow and stabbed and strangled her to death. He buried her in a shallow grave, and returned several times. By the time he dug up her rotting corpse, intending to nail it to a tree in a sick parody of crucifixion, her body was in an advanced state of decomposition, and was too heavy for him to prop up against the tree. His impromptu art project failed.

August 21 was a busy night for Kürten. First he attacked a housewife on her way home from a county fair, stabbing her in the back. Then he stabbed 8-year-old Anna Goldhausen and 38-year-old Gustav Kornblum ... and all of this within half an hour. None of the attacks were fatal, but the people of Düsseldorf were thrown into a panic.

Even with an increased police presence on the streets of the city, the "Düsseldorf Ripper" struck again three days later. Foster-sisters Louise Lenzen, age 14, and Gertrude Hamacher, age 5, were attacked on their way home from the market. Kürten ambushed them in a garden. He choked them both into unconsciousness, then slit their throats and stabbed Louise four times in the back.

The next day, Kürten assaulted Gertrude Schulte. The woman survived the attack, and was able to give police a description of her assailant. She described him as a pleasant-looking male, around forty years old. This did not do much to narrow down the list of suspects.

By now, the press was whipping the public into a frenzy of paranoia, and Kürten was enjoying every moment of the mass hysteria. A servant girl, Ida Reuter, 31 years old, was raped and killed September 30. Kürten invited her to a café for a beer, and then they took a stroll along the banks of the Rhine. There, he smashed her skull repeatedly with a hammer, and sexually assaulted her corpse. Six weeks later, on October 11, he beat 22-year-old Elizabeth Dörrier, also a servant girl, into unconsciousness with a hammer, and raped her. She died the next morning, mercifully never having regained consciousness.

Around sundown on November 7, Kürten committed his final murder. He approached Gertrude Albermann as the 5-year-old was playing in the street outside her home. He simply took her hand and led her away, telling her he wanted to show her something. He brought her to an abandoned factory, where he sexually assaulted her and strangled her. Then he stabbed her thirty-six times in the chest and head.

Two days later, suffused with yet another victory, Kürten sent an anonymous letter to a local newspaper. He'd hidden Gertrude's body under some loose rubble, he wrote, and he offered directions to the five-year-old's makeshift grave. He included a bonus, too: a hand-drawn map of the location of Maria Hahn's grave. Both corpses were found, which racheted the press up to a fever pitch. Gertrude was found lying face down in a patch of nettles near the factory wall the same day the letter made it into the newspaper. Maria's badly decomposed body was dug up November 14.

Kürten attacked several more victims over the winter and into the spring of 1930. None of the attacks were fatal, but the entire country was in an agony of suspense. The investigation of the "Düsseldorf Ripper" was now spearheaded by Detective Chief Inspector Ernst Gennat of Berlin's Alexanderplatz (Germany's version of Scotland Yard). Gennat realized that the letter to the newspaper was a sign that the murderer's grasp on his impulses was slipping.

He was right.

On May 14, 1930, Kürten met a young woman named Maria Büdlick. Discovering that she was unemployed, he offered her a place to stay. He took her to his apartment and offered her some hot cocoa. He was hoping to have sex with her, but she refused. He said hey, no hard feelings, and agreed to help her find somewhere else to stay. He took her back to the train station, but then dragged her into the nearby Grafenburger woods and raped her before letting her go.

A week later, on May 21, Kürten was startled to see Büdlick back at his apartment building. (He'd let her go, he later said, because she had offered no resistance to his rape, and because he didn't think she could find her way back to the neighborhood.) He was even more startled to see that she was with DCI Ernst Gennat. Büdlick had been afraid to report the attack to the police, so instead, she had written a detailed letter to a friend. The letter was misdelivered to a total stranger, who opened it, read it, and went straight to the authorities. Gennat tracked down Büdlick, who agreed to tell him the location of Kürten's apartment. When he saw the two, Kürten slipped quietly out of the building's hallway and went immediately to the restaurant where his wife worked.

Kürten was a monster, to be sure. But he honestly held his wife, Auguste, in high regard. He knew that, now that Gennat knew his identity, it would be only a matter of time before he was arrested for Büdlick's rape. He told Auguste that he had to lay low for a while. He snuck back into the apartment, grabbed a few things, then holed up in a rented room for a couple of days.

On Friday, May 23, two detectives showed up at Auguste's workplace. They escorted her back to the apartment and searched the place. Shortly after they left, Peter returned home. Auguste told him that the police had just left. Peter confessed that he'd tried to rape another girl the previous summer. Faced with the suddenly real possibility that Peter would be jailed yet again for these assaults, Auguste broke down. She proposed that they both commit suicide.

Peter talked her out of it, saying that he had a much better plan. By this time, there was a massive reward being offered for the capture of the "Düsseldorf Ripper". Peter confessed everything to her, and ended by convincing her to turn him in to the authorities. The reward money would take care of her financially when he could not. He insisted, too, that turning him in would not be a betrayal of their marriage. In fact, he pointed out, she would be doing a good deed for society by aiding in his capture. Reluctantly, Auguste agreed that this all made sense. Peter and Auguste made plans to meet the next day at 3 pm outside St. Rochus Church, where Peter would turn himself in.

On May 24, 1930, Auguste Kürten took the police to the church. Peter was waiting for them there, and he quietly surrendered.

Once Kürten was in custody, the floodgates opened, and he confessed to everything. He took full responsibility for the "Düsseldorf Ripper" attacks of 1929-1930. He also confessed to the 1913 murders of Gertrud Franken and Christine Klein—murders that the police hadn't previously connected to the Düsseldorf attacks. Kürten also copped to nearly two dozen arsons ... and, bizarrely, the slaughter of a swan.

"I used to stroll through the Hoftgarten very often," Kürten told the investigators, "and in the spring of 1930 I noticed a swan sleeping at the edge of the lake. I cut its throat. The blood spurted up from the stump and I drank it."

Kürten held nothing back in his confession. He figured that the more he confessed to, the greater the financial benefits would be for Auguste. He seemed to take great pleasure in reliving every moment of his depravity. (The stenographers who were taking notes? Not so much.) He admitted that he'd been sexually aroused by the sight of blood since childhood. He also claimed to have drunk the blood of many of his victims. Once this gory tidbit got out, the press hung a new handle on him. Peter Kürten was no longer the "Düsseldorf Ripper." Now, his nickname was the "Vampire of Düsseldorf."

Kürten confessed to 79 acts of crime in all. On April 13, 1931, his trial for nine murders and seven attempted murders began. Through it all, Kürten gave the impression of a successful businessman, appearing in court every day in a well-tailored suit and a dapper haircut. At first, he tried to take back his extremely thorough confession, saying that he'd only wanted to make sure that the reward money would make Auguste financially secure. But over the next two months, the evidence against him piled up.

Peter Kürten never showed any remorse for his sadistic crimes. The jury took only 90 minutes to find him guilty on all counts. On April 22, he was convicted and sentenced to die by guillotine. Weirdo that he was, Kürten was thrilled by this. He asked the prison doctor excitedly, "Tell me, after my head is chopped off, will I still be able to hear, at least for a moment, the sound of my own blood gushing from the stump of my neck? That would be the pleasure to end all pleasures."

At dawn on July 2, 1931, Kürten may have discovered the answer to that morbid question. He was executed by guillotine in Cologne, Germany.

As soon as his head came off, scientists were all over it. His career as a serial killer had been so demented and ghoulish, investigators theorized that his brain had to be physically different, somehow, to account for his heinous crimes. So they decided to find out.

Kürten's skull was split in half and his brain was dissected in an attempt to discern the urges behind his savagery. The scientists found ... exactly nothing. Inside the bony confines of his skull, Peter Kürten was just like everyone else. But the scientists just couldn't let such an intriguing specimen go. Kürten's head was preserved, and ended up in a collection of oddities.

The afterlife saga of the head is a gross yet cool story in its own right. After World War II, the head was acquired by Arne Coward, an antiquities dealer in Hawaii. Coward collected antiques, but his true passion lay in getting his hands on instruments of torture: thumb screws, tongue tearers, nifty little trinkets like that. (It's said that Coward's experiences in a Nazi concentration camp honed his interest in all the ways human beings could be atrocious to each other.) Coward died in 1979, and his collection was put up for auction. Ripley's Believe It Or Not! bought the mummified head, and in 1990, they installed it in their Wisconsin Dells museum.

Kürten's head is now displayed in a glass case in the top floor of the museum, alongside an English warlock chest, an executioner's sword, and a mannequin depicting Elizabeth Bathory enjoying a rejuvenating dip in a tub of blood, in an exhibit that celebrates the dark and macabre. This corner of the museum has its own title: "The Darker Side of Ripley's". And it delivers. Kürten's head, impaled on a hook, revolves slowly and continuously, giving viewers a 360-degree rendition of the outside—and inside—of the gruesome relic. The head is perfectly preserved, down to the eyelashes. The eye sockets are hollow black pools of mystery. Inside, the nasal cavities and spinal cord and jaw are right there, split neatly down the middle, with teeth on either side. The brain—the perfectly normal-looking brain—is gone, but the rest of the inside of Kürten's head is on permanent display. It looks like an anatomy model in a particularly ambitious high school classroom, but a deep part of you knows that it isn't plastic. It's real. If you can bear to look at it for more than a few moments at a time, it looks ... wrong, somehow. We're not supposed to be able to see the inside of someone's head. But here we are.

Peter Kürten must have followed his head all the way from Germany, to Hawaii, to Wisconsin, because the museum definitely holds his presence. Museum employees have heard loud footsteps, bangs, muttered voices, all of which they attribute to Kürten. One employee had the frightening experience of hearing a horrendous crash from the front of the museum, as if the plate-glass display windows had suddenly shattered into confetti. When they raced to the front door, not a thing was out of place.

I visited the museum in June 2019 with several other investigators for a late-night ghost hunt. One of the docents, Penny, was kind enough to share her paranormal experiences with us. She's not intimidated by the mummified serial killer— far from it. On the contrary, she has an easy familiarity with Kürten's spirit.

"Peter is wherever Peter wants to be," she told us. He is not bound to the Darker Side exhibit, but wanders the entire building. "If you hear a bang, or someone walking, you just say, 'Hey Peter', and it'll just … go on its way," she said breezily. (For more of our conversation, please feel free to look up Lights Out #90: Ripley's Museum on YouTube. You can follow along with me as I explore the whole place.)

Peter's ghost is considered to be very protective of the museum and its exhibits. The Vampire of Düsseldorf seems to be quite comfortable in his final resting place … or at least the final resting place of his head.

Death in the Wisconsin Woods (1914)

The architect Frank Lloyd Wright was renowned for his innovative use of line and space. The early twentieth century was a fertile ground for Wright's inspired style. Wright's work radically changed architecture, in America and all over the world: he brought an informality and an openness not previously seen. Modern open floor plans, loft apartments, ranch houses—these are all heirs to Wright's influence.

Wright's work was so unique that a building designed by the master is instantly recognizable, with long, low, straight lines that harmonize with the landscape in which the building sits. This was on purpose; Wright pioneered a style of architecture that came to be known as the Prairie School movement. The horizontal lines of these structures were designed to evoke the broad, flat expanses of America's prairies. The Prairie School prized solid construction, thoughtful craftsmanship, and an aesthetic that harmonized the building and the landscape in which it sat.

It's interesting that several of Frank Lloyd Wright's houses have a touch of the macabre to them. Take the Ennis House, for example. It was built in 1924 in Los Feliz, California, for Charles and Mabel Ennis. Charles Ennis, who owned a men's department store, was a big fan of Mayan culture, so Wright designed the house using a style of architecture called Mayan Revival. The Ennis House was damaged by an earthquake in 1994, and in 2004, it suffered further by being pelted with torrential rains. A billionaire private owner has bought it and is refurbishing the stunning showplace.

And the Ennis House is, literally, a showplace—as in, it's

been in shows. In 1959, the house was featured in the classic horror film *House on Haunted Hill*. The movie, directed by William Castle (the man responsible for a string of B-rated flicks), starred Vincent Price as a sadistic millionaire who lures five guests to spend the night in his haunted house, promising them a large cash prize if they survive the night. This wasn't the Ennis House's only time in the spotlight, either. The atmospheric exterior was used as the set of a mansion occupied by evil vampires in the TV series *Buffy the Vampire Slayer*, and the interior was used for the apartment of Rick Deckard (played by Harrison Ford) in *Blade Runner*.

A couple of Frank Lloyd Wright-designed houses actually have their own resident ghosts. Susan Lawrence Dana was an independent woman living in Springfield, Illinois, who inherited a huge fortune from her father. Despite her wealth, Susie was an unhappy woman; she suffered the loss of two infant children and both her first and second husbands, in addition to other family members.

In 1902, Susie decided to have a massive home built, to facilitate the entertaining she planned to do. Susie loved parties, especially during the Christmas season, and every year she held an open house at Christmas and feted her staff and their children, and others in the community. She also held séance parties in her homes, opening it to spiritualist groups. She tapped a young Frank Lloyd Wright to bring his magic to her life. She gave him a blank check, backed by her then-enormous fortune, to design not only the home, but also the furniture within its walls.

Unfortunately, the money didn't last forever. Susie Dana ended up with a magnificent home, but she died penniless in an insane asylum in 1946. The furniture was offered for sale to cover her debts, but no one wanted it because it looked uncomfortable. (Let's face it, no one ever accused Wright of designing a comfy, overstuffed armchair. It just wasn't his style.) A publisher, Charles Thomas, bought the house and its contents in 1944, and moved his offices into the sprawling house. The state of Illinois bought the mansion from Thomas in 1981 and restored it to reflect the glory days of Susie's early twentieth-century residence. It's now a historic site, named the Dana-Thomas House to honor both of the mansion's owners.

Susie Dana loved the house that had been designed expressly for her. She believed that aesthetics could enhance one's personal life—if you surround yourself with beauty, your experience of life will also be beautiful—so she has never left her magnificent home. She drifts around the house, putting in appearances especially around Christmas, her favorite holiday. (For detailed examples of the hauntings at the Dana-Thomas House, please see my book *Spirits of Christmas: The Dark Side of the Holidays.*)

Or consider Fallingwater, the stunning home that Wright designed for Edgar J. Kaufmann, president of Kaufmann's department stores. Fallingwater is a stunning work of architecture. Built between 1936 and 1939, the house is nestled into the primeval landscape of the Allegheny Mountains of southwestern Pennsylvania. The Kaufmanns asked Wright to build a mansion in which they could enjoy a waterfall in Bear Run. Imagine their surprise—and delight—when Wright designed their house to balance *over* the waterfall. Instead of admiring the falls from afar, the Kaufmanns would get up close and personal with nature.

But Fallingwater, too, was visited by tragedy. Edgar Kaufmann was a serial cheater, and on September 7, 1952, his wife, Liliane, died of an overdose of sleeping pills in the master bedroom—a bedroom in which she slept alone. At the time of her death, her husband was carrying on with the latest in a string of mistresses. The overdose was ruled an accident, but some theorize that Liliane died by suicide, and a broken heart. She is said to haunt Fallingwater. She manifests as a melancholy figure in a white gown, who stares pensively out of the window of the bedroom in which she died, gazing out at the rushing waterfall.

Yet another Frank Lloyd Wright house that saw heartbreak is the Bradley House in Kankakee, Illinois. B. Harley Bradley, heir to the David Bradley Manufacturing Company of Chicago, married Anna M. Hickox, herself an heiress to a real estate business, in 1897. Three years later, Anna and her brother

Warren Hickox Jr. hired Frank Lloyd Wright to build adjoining houses for them.

B. Harley and Anna and their adopted daughter Margaret lived in the massive Bradley House for about eleven and a half years, from the spring of 1901 to the fall of 1912. Then financial misfortune struck the family. The founder of the farm-implement company, David Bradley, the family's patriarch, had died in 1899. His descendants had tried to carry on the business, but the firm was bought out by Sears, Roebuck and Company in 1910. The big conglomerate kept the name, but other than that, they took total control of the company, and David's heirs were left out in the cold. B. Harley was an invalid to begin with, due to a childhood illness, so he was not one of the Bradleys that was allowed to keep working for his grandfather's company after the takeover. He and Anna sold their home to a wealthy Iowan named A. E. Cook in September 1912. They basically traded the mansion for $1 and 522 acres of Cook's land in western Iowa (and Cook had land to spare). B. Harley, Anna, Margaret, and B. Harley's retired parents, who'd been living with them, all moved to Onawa, Iowa, in search of a fresh start.

But Bradley's money troubles followed him west. In July 1914, the 43 year old went to Chicago on what he told Anna was a business trip. Instead, he bought a .32 caliber pistol for $10 at a sporting goods store in the Loop. He wrote a letter to Anna, posted it, then came back to his hotel room at 10 pm that evening. He put the pistol under his pillow and slept on the idea. The next morning, Monday, July 13, he woke up around 9 am. He lay there thinking for a while, then propped himself up with two pillows, stuck the gun barrel against his head, and pulled the trigger. The shot went through both temples and blinded him, but didn't kill him right away. He lingered until 5 pm that evening, dying at St. Luke's Hospital. In response to his letter, Anna rushed to Chicago on the 6 o'clock overnight train, not knowing that he was already dead by the time she and Margaret boarded.

This tragedy was trumpeted in Chicago papers for one day, then was pushed off the front page by other news. The headlines appeared in the newspapers almost exactly one month before another newsworthy event in Frank Lloyd Wright's life ... but we'll get to that soon.

Fate and misfortune weren't finished with the Bradley House. A. E. Cook himself fell on hard times, and had to sell the mansion. It was purchased by Joseph H. Dodson, affectionately known as the Birdman. Dodson was rabidly passionate about birds, hence the nickname. He put out dozens of birdbaths and feeders on the property, and turned the ornate stables and carriage house into a factory for the manufacture of Dodson Bird Houses, which he sold across the nation. By his estimate, his yard was home to three or four hundred species of bird every spring and summer of the thirty-four years he owned the property. He died at the house, which he named Bird Lodge, in the fall of 1949.

A local car dealer and his wife, Ed and Alice Bergeron, owned the house for a short while. Then, in January 1953, they sold it to a gay couple, Marvin Hammack and Ray Schimel. The couple repurposed Wright's mansion into an inn, which they called Yesteryear. The inn's restaurant became famous for its exquisite cuisine, with diners coming from as far away as Chicago and St. Louis for a prime rib dinner.

The innkeepers owned the property for the next three decades, but they both fell ill in the early 1980s. In April 1984, they decided to retire to property they owned in Fort Lauderdale. They sold the restaurant to a local businessman and his partner. The new owners tried to make a go of the restaurant business, but they hadn't owned it even ten months before they had to declare bankruptcy. In March 1985, the electricity was shut off during the Friday lunch hour. Six months later, a reporter from the *Chicago Tribune* wrote that the Bradley House had "deteriorated into a vacant, cold, and musty-smelling building."

But! It was still a Frank Lloyd Wright house, and people wanted to save it. In 1986, the Bradley House got a new lease on life. It was bought by Stephen Small, a 40-year-old executive whose family controlled a conglomerate called Mid America Media. Small was a family man, a nice guy, according to all who knew him. He and his wife intended to restore the grand old mansion. They started immediately, and began with the badly deteriorated roof.

But on September 2, 1987, Small got a phone call in the middle of the night at his nearby home. The voice on the other end of the line told him that burglars were breaking into the Bradley House. Small raced to the scene, where kidnappers handcuffed him and shoved a stocking cap over his face. They drove Small to a wooded area about twelve miles southeast of town. There, they buried him alive in a homemade box. They forced him into the 3 foot by 6 foot box, and dropped in five candy bars, a jug of water, a flashlight, a pack of gum, and another light hooked up to two car batteries. Then they shovelled three feet of sandy earth onto his prison. Intending to keep Small alive for the $1 million ransom, the kidnappers rigged up a length of PVC pipe that ran from the box up through the dirt like a periscope.

Unfortunately, the pipe didn't work. Small suffocated to death in the box. At the trial, the medical examiner testified that he'd probably survived for no more than three or four hours.

Police and FBI investigators discovered Small's shallow grave about 72 hours after he'd been taken. By that time, they had the kidnappers in custody: 30-year-old Daniel Edwards, a local coke dealer, and his 26-year-old girlfriend, Nancy Rish, a cashier at Kroger. The kidnappers were rank amateurs—the ransom demands were made from gas station pay phones, which the police traced with ease. And Edwards had built the plywood box in his garage, sealed the seams with white caulk ... and then threw his caulk-smeared work gloves in the garbage. The jury listened to a recording of Small's voice, screaming in panic as he slammed his hands on the roof of his makeshift coffin over and over in a desperate search for air. Edwards was convicted of first-degree murder. A few days later, he was sentenced to death. Rish, tried separately, got life in prison.

But even with this horrific scenario, the Bradley House isn't haunted. However, almost exactly one month after B. Harley Bradley shot himself through both temples, another Wright home was visited by tragedy.

And this time, Wright himself was caught up in the drama. Frank Lloyd Wright, like many artistic geniuses, had a tempestuous love life. He was married three times, and had dalliances on the side. He married Catherine Lee "Kitty" Tobin in 1889; he was 22, she was 18. Within five years, the couple had welcomed four of their eventual six children—and Wright had two more children with his third wife, Olga Lazovich Hinzenburg. He met Olga while still married to his second wife, Maude "Miriam" Noel, who had been his mistress while he was married to Kitty (you remember, his first wife. I told you things were complicated). His marriage to Miriam lasted less than a year, due to her addiction to morphine.

In 1903, while he was still married to Wife Number One, Wright was designing a house for Edwin Cheney, a neighbor of his in Oak Park, Illinois. Wright fell hard for Cheney's wife, Martha Borthwick Cheney, nicknamed Mamah. Mamah found her intellectual equal in Wright. A thoroughly modern woman, a feminist with broad-ranging interests, Mamah was a good match for Wright. (Too bad they were both married. To other people.) In 1909, Wright and Mamah Cheney hared off to Europe, sans their respective spouses and children. While they were there, Edwin Cheney granted Mamah a divorce, but Kitty Wright refused to divorce Frank.

When the couple returned to the States in October 1910, Wright asked his mother to buy some land for him in Spring Green, Wisconsin. She bought some property adjacent to land already owned by her family, the Lloyd-Joneses, and in May 1911, Wright began work on a home for himself and his mistress, a house he named Taliesin.

Wright hoped to keep his relationship with Mamah out of the public eye, but if he thought that moving to rural Wisconsin was going to accomplish that, he was sorely mistaken. The upright citizens of Spring Green were not thrilled that Wright had chosen their town for his studio and his mistress's home. (Wright and Cheney called their home Taliesin—the press named it the "Love Cottage.") The whole affair was terrifically scandalous. Criticism rained down on Wright for what the townspeople saw as his immoral relationship with Cheney. But the brilliant, eccentric architect was deeply in love, and really didn't give a damn what anyone else thought.

This idyllic paradise in the Wisconsin woods was not to last, however.

Wright hired workers—draftsmen, landscape gardeners, household help—to staff the mansion for Mamah's comfort. Included in the employee roster was a married couple, Julian and Gertrude Carlton. Julian, a 31-year-old native of Barbados, waited tables and did housework at the mansion. Gertrude did most of the cooking.

Julian was disliked by the other employees on the estate. (It may have had its roots in race—there just weren't many Black people in rural Wisconsin at that time.) Over the summer, he'd been harassed by his fellow employees, and at the beginning of August, there had been an argument over the saddling of a horse. Mamah was aware of the friction in the household, and had given notice that the couple was to leave her employment. This fueled Julian's paranoia, and even his wife said later that he'd taken to keeping a hatchet in a bag next to his bed. The couple's last day at the estate was to be August 15, 1914.

On August 15, Wright was in Chicago on business, designing Midway Gardens. The staff at the estate were going about their duties. Gertrude fixed lunch for Mamah, her children John and Martha, and the rest of the employees. Then she planned to pack her and Julian's belongings, as they were to board a train back to Chicago that night.

Meanwhile, Julian had plans of his own.

Lunch was served to the family and staff at noon. Mamah and the children ate on the porch. At the other end of a 25-foot-long corridor, the employees ate in their dining room. The meal began with soup ... and ended with wholesale slaughter.

Julian served soup to the staff. The workers—draftsman Herbert Fritz, gardener David Lindblom, draftsman Emil Brodelle, workman Thomas Brunker, and carpenter William Weston, along with Ernest Weston, William's 13-year-old son—tucked into the first course. As they ate, they noticed something weird. Fritz later described it.

"We heard a swish as though water was thrown through the screen door. Then we saw some fluid coming under the door. It looked like dishwater. It spread out all over the floor."

What Fritz mistook for dishwater was actually gasoline. Julian locked the door to the staff dining room and lit the gas on fire. He served soup to Mamah and the children, then went to the kitchen, found Gertrude, and told her to leave the house.

With the fire spreading quickly, Julian went back to the porch. Mamah, trying to escape the smoke and flames, stuck her head out of the porch window, gasping for breath. Julian was waiting with his hatchet. He brought it down, slicing Mamah's neck and crushing her skull. Next, Julian attacked 12-year-old John, chopping his head open. Then he turned the hatchet on Martha, nine years old. He left the butchered corpses to the flames, and went to finish his grisly work.

The staff dining room was now fully engulfed in fire. Finding the door locked, Herbert Fritz jumped out of the window next to where he'd been sitting, and rolled down the hillside, smothering the flames that were consuming his clothes and hair. Meanwhile, his co-workers had forced the door open, only to be met by Julian and his hatchet. Anyone who escaped the inferno then faced the blade.

David Lindblom and William Weston managed to evade Julian's attack. They found Fritz, and the three wounded, burned men made their way half a mile to the nearest house with a phone to call for help. First responders to the scene found the bodies of Mamah, her two children, and workers Emil Brodelle and Thomas Brunker, and Ernest Weston. Lindblom later died of his burn injuries.

Meanwhile, Julian had retreated—into the burning house. He had hidden in the fireproof furnace room in the basement. With him was a vial of hydrochloric acid; he'd planned to commit suicide if the heat above him became too much to bear. By the time police found him, he had drunk the acid. Julian was nearly lynched on the spot, but he was taken instead to the jail in Dodgeville. His esophagus was ravaged by the acid, and it took him seven weeks to die of starvation. He never recovered enough to stand trial for the mass murder.

Wright and Edwin Cheney returned on the same train from Chicago to deal with the wreckage of their lives. Cheney took his children's bodies back to Chicago for burial. Wright, devastated at Mamah's death, buried her without a funeral in an unmarked grave. He couldn't bear to be reminded of his horrific loss.

In the aftermath of the attack, firefighters took the badly burned, dead and dying victims to a cottage on the grounds of the estate. It is this building, named Tan-y-Deri, that is home to Mamah Borthwick Cheney's ghost. She is seen here, and much like her counterpart Liliane Kaufmann at Fallingwater, she wears a flowing white gown. Her presence is said to be peaceful, but restless, as if she is still reliving her awful death and the loss of her children.

Other manifestations of the energy of the tragedy include windows and doors that open and close by themselves, and lights that turn themselves on and off with no human hand on the switch. Caretakers often report closing the cottage up securely for the night, only to return the next morning to find the windows and doors all standing open.

Such is the lasting energy of the tragic loss of life at Frank Lloyd Wright's Taliesin.

Rival Priests (1915)

Morning Mass in the Catholic Church is normally a peaceful time, an opportunity for quiet reflection. But on August 27, 1915, in the chapel on the second floor of St. Mary's Hall, Bishop Patrick Heffron had his private time rudely interrupted. Father Louis Michael Lesches came into the chapel and shot the bishop twice as he knelt in prayer.

Fr. Lesches had been aching for an assignment to his own parish for years. But Bishop Heffron, his superior, refused to give him a posting. He found Fr. Lesches "eccentric, peculiar, and unreliable", unfit to serve as a pastor. The mentally unstable Lesches seethed under this slight. Bishop Heffron was a man of strong character and iron will, someone who did what he thought was best for his flock whether others liked it or not. Once he'd made up his mind, he could not be swayed.

Years of conflict between the two men finally boiled over into violence. Lesches came into the bishop's private chapel armed with a Smith & Wesson revolver. He fired four times, and two of those shots found their mark. The second round smashed into the bishop's thigh. The third shot hit the altar, but by the fourth shot, Lesches was close enough to aim directly at Heffron's heart. Heffron threw out his left arm to deflect the shot. The final shot, delivered so close that the bishop's vestments had powder burns on them, lodged in Heffron's chest. Lesches fled the chapel and retreated to his room, where he was arrested shortly after the attack.

Bishop Heffron, tough old goat that he was, survived the shooting, and testified at Lesches' trial. Father Lesches was acquitted by reason of insanity, and spent the rest of his life in the State Hospital for the Dangerous Insane at St. Peter, Minnesota. He died there in 1943 at the age of 84. He'd spent almost 28 years in the asylum. Heffron, 56 years old at the time of the shooting, recovered quickly and lived another twelve years, dying of cancer at the age of 68.

From then on, whenever something weird happened at St. Mary's College, it was blamed on Fr. Lesches. And plenty of weird stuff happened. Apparently, being locked up didn't stop Fr. Lesches' vindictive streak. Faculty members died premature deaths in strange accidents after the attack on Bishop Heffron. The most bizarre of these was the death of Father Edward Lynch.

Fr. Lynch and Fr. Lesches had once been roommates, but since Lynch was good friends with Bishop Heffron, Lesches soon came to consider him an enemy. While they were roommates, Lynch had mentioned that he was a big sports fan. The unbalanced Lesches had snapped that Lynch would burn in hell for his sinful love of athletics.

On May 15, 1931, a nun cleaning rooms discovered Lynch's burned body lying face-up in bed. The bed wasn't even singed, but the priest's body had been charred, and a burned Bible lay nearby. The coroner, lacking any other explanation, ruled that Lynch had been reading his Bible in bed, and had been electrocuted by a faulty lamp when he reached up to turn off the light. But 110 volts of electricity is not enough to burn a body so completely.

The superstitious on campus swore there was a supernatural connection, that Fr. Lesches was somehow responsible. The explanation had to have a paranormal element … because at the time of Lynch's death, Michael Lesches was a patient at St. Peter Hospital for the Dangerous Insane.

The ghost of Fr. Lesches, still bitter and insane after death, still haunts Saint Mary's College. He is especially active in Heffron Hall, the dormitory built in 1921 and named in honor of his arch-nemesis. The antagonistic phantom concentrates his energy on the third floor, causing cold spots and anomalous breezes. There have also been a few face-to-face confrontations. One student, startled by the priest's sudden appearance, reflexively threw a punch—and broke his hand when the punch hit the wall behind the ghost.

"The Devil Made Me Do It" (1925)

Every serial killer needs a cool nickname. Martha Wise became known as "The Borgia of America." But other than her habit of poisoning people, Martha had very little in common with a glamorous Italian Renaissance noblewoman.

Martha Hasel was born in the mid-1880s in Medina County, Ohio, and lived in a town aptly named Hardscrabble. This basically describes Martha's entire life. She married a man named Albert Wise, who was horribly abusive. He beat her, and forced her to go out and plow in their fields the day after she'd given birth to one of their children. About the only bright spot in Martha's life was when a funeral was held; that gave her a welcome chance to escape the house and do some socializing with her neighbors. She said herself that she didn't miss a funeral in twenty years.

Martha was a plain, crabbed-looking woman with pretty serious health issues. She probably suffered from undiagnosed epilepsy, and she also survived a bout of meningitis in her youth. Her strange behavior included fits and foaming at the mouth, which understandably freaked out her neighbors. Her habit of wandering the area late at night also raised eyebrows, as did the fact that if someone spoke to her in her wanderings, she tended to bark at them rather than answer with words. In spite of her idiosyncrasies, she was respected in the community as a person who readily helped out when there was sickness in a family.

Albert Wise died suddenly in 1923, leaving Martha with their four children. Martha, free to do as she wished for the first time in years, fell in love with Walter Johns. It looked like the

40-year-old widow had finally found happiness after years of abuse … but that's not the way things turned out.

Martha's family had a problem with Walter. Specifically, they had a problem with the fact that he was much younger than Martha. They weren't willing to overlook this May-October romance, and were pretty blunt in their criticism of Martha. They called her a cradle-robber, and ridiculed her for the difference in their ages.

Martha soon got sick and tired of her family casing on her. She began to act out. A rash of petty burglaries swept through the town, as the townsfolk of Hardscrabble started to notice things missing—jewelry, heirlooms, small knickknacks, even family portraits. More seriously, at the same time there was a wave of arson. Haystacks went up in flames, and ten barns were torched. Livestock was lost in several of the fires.

About three weeks before New Year's, Sophie Hasel, Martha's mother, died suddenly. Martha did her grieving, went to the funeral, then moved on. She fixed a feast for the Geinke family, her relatives, on New Year's Day 1925. (Lily Geinke, Martha's aunt, married to Fred, was Sophie Hasel's sister.) Fred Geinke, his wife, their six children, and several other relatives sat down to a meal with all the trimmings: roast suckling pig, complete with an apple in its mouth, bowl after bowl of vegetables, four kinds of pie …

The feast also included a hearty helping of arsenic.

Several hours after the family pushed back from the table, groaning with pleasure at the meal, a neighbor woman heard agonized screams coming from the Geinke house. She went to see what was wrong, then raced to Martha's house for help … as Martha was known to the entire valley as "Widow Wise", who tenderly cared for the sick and ailing of Hardscrabble. Martha got the stricken family into bed and was bathing their foreheads with cool water when two doctors arrived. The physicians gave everyone emetics, assuming that the big meal had given the family food poisoning. Neighbors rushed two of the children, Marie and Rudolph, to the Medina County hospital. They seemed the sickest, but they recovered.

Other family members were not so lucky.

On February 9, Fred Geinke, who had seemed to be getting better, took a turn for the worse and died. Lily, his wife, was still bedridden, but she sent for Martha to make Fred's funeral arrangements. Ever the dutiful niece, Martha cleaned the house and cooked a good solid spread for the neighbors who came to pay their respects. After all, funerals were social affairs, a chance for the living to come together to honor the deceased. For some, like Martha, a funeral was the highlight of their social calendar. After the last mourner left, Lily thanked her niece for stepping up in a time of need. "I don't know what I'd do without you," she told Martha.

Three days later, Lily too was dead. She'd been expected to recover, but she relapsed and died in agony before the doctor could get to the house.

Throughout all of this misfortune in Hardscrabble—the mysterious deaths, the arson, the burglaries—County Prosecutor Joseph Seymour and Sheriff George Roshon were keeping a close eye on the situation. After yet another sudden death in the Geinke family, they began to do a little digging. Both men realized that the poisoning victims were all in the Geinke or Hasel households. They'd heard, too, that Martha had told her children not to drink any water at either house.

Another fact that came to the men's attention was that Martha had recently bought some arsenic, ostensibly to rid her home of rats. Seymour ordered the exhumation of Lily Geinke's body. The subsequent autopsy revealed enough arsenic in her system to kill a dozen people.

Seymour wasn't stupid. He questioned Martha about the poisoning, which she categorically denied. He got no information from her, so he changed his tactics. He suggested she take a trip to Cleveland. She was suffering from a lingering infection on her arm, which because of her health issues and the stress she was under, was slow to heal. Seymour thought it might be a good idea to get the arm looked at by a doctor in a larger town than Hardscrabble. He said sympathetically that she'd been through a lot in the past several months, what with losing her mother, uncle, and aunt in such quick succession, and that she really deserved a rest.

Martha agreed. She could use a vacation. She left for Cleveland the next day, March 1. She was away for two weeks. And during those two weeks, there were no thefts reported, not a single barn burned down ... and no one mysteriously came down sick.

Sheriff Roshon picked Martha up from Cleveland, and he and Joseph Seymour confronted Martha with her crimes. The interrogation took place during a torrential rainstorm. Martha seemed on edge, her nerves shredded by the incessant noise of the rain on the tin roof of the building. Seymour, knowing that Martha was deeply religious, used the atmosphere to his advantage.

"Listen, Martha, listen to the raindrops on the roof," Seymour urged. "They are the voice of God, Martha. Listen to what they are saying ... you did it, Martha."

Martha resisted at first, then her nerve broke and she confessed.

"It was the devil who told me to do it. He came to me while I was in the kitchen baking bread. He came to me while I was working in the fields. He followed me everywhere." She also confessed to the thefts and the arson incidents. "I like fires," she explained. "They were red and bright, and I loved to see the flames shooting up into the sky."

Seymour and Roshon also discovered that Martha had bought 960 grains of arsenic from a druggist in Elyria. The poisonings she'd carried out thus far had only taken a few dozen grains. Martha Wise had enough arsenic on hand to kill everyone in Hardscrabble.

She explained this compulsion too. "I liked their funerals. I could get dressed up and see folks and talk to them. I didn't miss a funeral in twenty years. The only fun I ever had was after I kilt people."

Martha pled insanity. Her boyfriend, Walter Johns, tried to help her insanity plea by testifying that Martha had "barked like a dog" during sex. However, the jury found her sane, and guilty of first-degree murder.

She was sent to Marysville Reformatory for Women, where she became a model prisoner. Her sentence was eventually reduced to second-degree murder.

Martha spent almost half her life in prison. She was granted parole in 1962, when she was nearing 80. She didn't ask for it, and probably didn't even want it at that point. She was released, but prison authorities ran into a snag: they couldn't find anyone willing to take the old woman in. Her children refused to have anything to do with her. (Martha's four children, Gertrude, Kenneth, Lester, and Everett, were farmed out to relatives when their mother was sentenced to life in prison.) Prison officials contacted a halfway house for the indigent elderly, hoping to place Martha there. But Muriel Worthing, the owner, backed out of the arrangement, saying that since the home served food to the public, it would look really bad to have a poisoner living there. Martha was returned to Marysville, and died there on June 28, 1971. She is buried in the prison cemetery.

Myrtle Hill Cemetery in Valley City, Ohio, is home to a striking monument that has, over the years, earned the nickname "the Witch's Ball." It's a large, dark gray sphere of polished granite, which sits atop a stone bearing the name "Stoskopf." It's not actually a gravestone, as no one is buried directly underneath it. It's simply a family plot marker. The Stoskopf family originally bought seven plots at Myrtle Hill Cemetery. They ended up using four of them. George Stoskopf, his wife Alma, their daughter, also named Alma, and her husband Joseph Toth are all buried near the marker.

The Witch's Ball is considered by local lore to refer to the crimes of Martha Wise. So how did the Stoskopf monument become associated with the notorious poisoner? Well, several of Martha's victims, including Sophie Hasel and Lily Geinke, are buried in Myrtle Hill Cemetery, pretty close to the stone. And the Stoskopf monument looks very imposing, and kind of creepy, especially if you buy into the lore that a witch (read: Martha Wise) is buried under it. It's said that even nature is afraid of the Witch's Ball, and that trees won't drop their leaves near the stone. (This is, of course, setting aside the fact that there aren't any trees within fifty yards of the marker, and the closest trees are evergreens.) Also, the stone is said to be cold during the day and warm to the touch at night. (Again, boring old physics comes up with an explanation. The polished granite starts out cool after the dark hours of the night. It soaks up the sun's heat during the day, and takes a while to warm up. By the time it gets up to temperature, the sun has gone down, and the granite returns that heat.)

A shadowy female figure is said to wander Myrtle Hill Cemetery, but witnesses agree that the ghost is more likely Sophie Hasel, rather than her daughter Martha Wise.

Wrong Place, Wrong Time (1948)

A first date on a hot summer night. The warm June air is redolent with possibilities. But for two young people, their first date on June 24, 1948, ended in unsolved murder.

Mary Jane Reed and Stanley Skridla both worked at DeKalb/Ogle Telephone Company. Skridla, 28, was a lineman, and Reed, 17, was a switchboard operator. Reed was excited about their date, in spite of their age difference. She wouldn't let that bother her. Skridla was a Navy vet from the big city of Rockford, and Mary Jane was looking forward to showing off her handsome new fella.

Their first date took them to several bars in Oregon, Illinois that night. At the end of the evening, they drove out to County Farm Road in Skridla's Buick for a little action on the popular lover's lane.

They were never seen alive again.

Stan Skridla's body was found the next day on County Farm Road, lying face down in a ditch. He had been shot low in the belly and dragged into the grass to die. Police later found five .32-caliber casings. About an hour later, his Buick turned up roughly a mile away. Except for a lipstick-smeared cigarette in the car, there was no sign of Mary Jane.

Skridla was buried on June 28. The next day, a man found Mary Jane's body in a patch of weeds along Silica Road. That area had been searched several times; Mary Jane's father passed the site every day on his way to work. She was found by a truck driver—the height of his cab meant that he could see over the weeds. She had been shot in the back of the head with what looked like the same caliber of gun used to kill Skridla.

The case has never been solved. Robbery didn't seem to be a motive, as Skridla still had his wallet and Mary Jane was wearing her mother's wedding ring. Investigations didn't get very far; they mostly led to dead ends.

The case went cold, and in spite of being reopened in early 2006, is still a mystery. One of the people interested in seeing justice done is Mike Arians. He was led to the case by Mary Jane herself.

Arians bought the Roadhouse, which in a previous incarnation as the Stenhouse, was possibly the last place Mary Jane Reed stopped before she and Skridla were killed. When Arians bought the place in the late 1990s, it was called the Seven Seas, and it was in pretty rough shape. But Mike had faith in the potential of the old building.

"When I first walked into the place, it had a very powerful, almost warm, inviting, cordial type of feeling," he said. "It's like it came to life before my eyes. I walked in here, and I could see how things were and how things used to be and … the potential, and it just kind of grabbed me."

He started remodeling the building, and would sleep there overnight while the renovations were going on. Many of those nights were peaceful. But at other times, the place was alive with weird noises. A couple of times, a stack of plates or a pile of pots and pans would collapse in the middle of the night, filling the air with a cacophony of noise.

The disturbances continued after the Roadhouse opened. Mike and his staff had a theory: they guessed that the paranormal activity was the work of one Esther Stenhouse. She and her husband had owned the pub in the 1930s and 40s. It was rumored that Esther had died of a heart attack in the bathtub upstairs, and her ghost still oversaw the establishment.

But the "Esther" theory didn't explain all of the peculiar occurrences that disrupted the day-to-day of the Roadhouse. The jukebox would spontaneously play the song "After Sunrise", which features the beautiful wordless voice of a female artist. Mike started seeing references to Mary Jane Reed everywhere. He got a letter from the Illinois Environmental Protection Agency on stormwater management, which was signed by a

Mary Reed. A fax sent by an equipment company included the name of the employee who'd sent it: Mary Jane.

And then there was the flower delivery on November 15.

One day, a delivery man showed up at the Roadhouse with a floral arrangement—for Mary Jane. No one knew where the arrangement had come from. No one had ordered it, and Mike wasn't there at the time, so the driver was sent on his way. Mike never did find out who sent flowers to the Roadhouse on November 15 … Mary Jane's birthday.

The weirdness was too much for some of the employees. One bartender quit outright, saying that the vibe in the place at night creeped her out. One of the waitresses saw an apparition in a hallway. Mike accepted the activity, as did his wife, June. The couple and their employees warmed to the idea that their resident ghost might not be Esther—it might be Mary Jane Reed.

"There's a presence at the Roadhouse that is very determined," Mike said.

Mike caught that determination. He started to research the cold case. What he found shook him deeply.

Mary Jane Reed was a popular girl, and had collected quite a few boyfriends by the tender age of seventeen. One of those boyfriends was Vince Varco, a chief deputy sheriff. Vince was married, but still ran around with Mary Jane. She, however, broke off the relationship … before Vince was ready for the fling to end. The afternoon before Mary Jane's date with Stan Skridla, Vince showed up at the Reed house. He pulled her outside and tried to talk her into taking him back. (He was, by all accounts, a bully, and not very subtle in his persuasion.) Mary Jane refused Vince, telling him she was dumping him for good in order to date Stan. Vince grabbed her by the arm. She struggled to get away, but he held onto her. Then he hit her several times before throwing her aside and taking off.

The next day, Stan Skridla was shot five times. Mary Jane was abducted, then murdered and her body thrown into a ditch. And the morning after that, according to Mike Arians' research, Vince Varco showed up for work without his .32 caliber service revolver, the same caliber used in both killings. (He said he'd sold it to some guy at a bar.) Coincidence? Maybe.

But the paperwork on the case, in the offices of the Ogle County Sheriff's Office, has some interesting things to say about Vince Varco. A report dated October 24, 1957, stated "Vincent Varco showed no signs of giving me any cooperation on the investigation. Varco was Chief Deputy of Ogle County and the investigation rested solely upon him." Another report noted the altercation at the Reed home, where Varco slapped Mary Jane several times because she wouldn't go out with him.

And there is a theory, pure conjecture decades later, based on simple psychology. It goes like this: Vince follows Stan and Mary Jane out to the lover's lane. When they park, Vince approaches them and shows his badge. He doesn't start shooting, not right away, because if someone does that, your instinct is to floor the gas pedal and get out of there. But he flashes his badge, telling Stan to get out of the car. Stan does, bracing for trouble, wondering what he's done to get a cop interested in him. Vince shoots Stan, then abducts Mary Jane and takes her to a secluded cabin near the Rock River. The hunt for Mary Jane after Stan's shooting was vast and intense, but her body wasn't found for four days. Maybe Vince took this time to try and argue Mary Jane around to his position. In the end, though, she still rejected him.

And was killed for it.

There are even more twists in this story. Bill Spencer, the former chief deputy sheriff of Ogle County, who investigated the murders, was quoted in the *Chicago Tribune* in 2003. One of his statements really stands out to someone interested in the case.

"Some people wouldn't talk at all," Spencer said. "They were afraid that they would become a victim, especially the women. They never did ever talk." This simple observation tells us quite a bit. Firstly, it seems to imply that the case was local to Oregon—meaning that Stan Skridla, from Rockford, was not the target. Secondly, there is an air of thinly-veiled threat. It would appear that there were people out there who knew exactly what happened to Mary Jane Reed, and that they were silenced.

There's an additional observation from another chief deputy sheriff, a man named William Burright. Burright stated that the

Reed-Skridla murder was a jealous lover thing. Knowing Vince Varco's history with Mary Jane, it's a reasonable conjecture. The newspapers picked up on this and ran with it. But Burright told the press that in an 18-month period, more than 150 persons who had been brought under suspicion had been questioned. 150 persons of interest? For a simple jealous lover case? This is deeply weird. It looks an awful lot like Burright was deliberately trying to muddy the waters ... maybe to hide his own involvement in the murders.

There's yet more weirdness in the case that directly involves Burright. Check this out: several months before the double murder, Burright helped put out a fire on the farm of Edwin Calhoun, located west of Oregon. The *Daily Chronicle* in DeKalb, Illinois, said that Burright was trying to keep a grass fire from destroying a garage in which barrels of gasoline were stored. One of the drums of gasoline exploded, and Burright's face and neck were badly burned.

Here's the interesting part: it was reported that on the day of the murders, Stan and Mary Jane had run into Burright sometime before heading to the Roadhouse. There was some sort of confrontation, and Mary Jane slapped Burright in the face. An insult like that, to an authority figure who was probably sensitive about his disfigurement, might have been a catalyst for revenge.

My friend Dean Thompson has investigated the Roadhouse for years. On December 26, 2009, he reached out to Mike Arians for the first time. Dean had some interesting information for Mike. He and Tim Schmuldt, another investigator, were checking out some local cemeteries. (Ghost hunters are not at all shy about poking around cemeteries. For one thing, they're easy access, and for another, they can sometimes lead to further investigations.)

At Daysville Cemetery, Dean had the feeling that "something bad happened over there"—he pointed west. He didn't mean in the woods that bordered the graveyard; his gut feeling drew him farther, past the woods. He also had a vision of a tree that was leaning at a severe angle. "It appeared larger than the other trees in the forest, like it didn't belong, and it was knocked over, pointing in the 2 o'clock position." At first, Dean put it down to an overactive imagination. But then, he heard the story of the Reed-Skridla murders.

Dean researched the story, and discovered that Stan Skridla's body had been found on County Farm Road. A search of a map revealed that when Dean stood in the cemetery and pointed over past the woods, he was pointing at the location of the murder. Stan's body was discovered just outside the woods on the other side of the river.

Dean fired off an email to Mike asking about the history of the murders. Mike took Dean on a tour of different locations that Mary Jane and Stan had visited on the night they were killed. The tour took Dean to a location that was never mentioned in the papers—a fishing cabin owned by Vince Varco, the cabin in which Mary Jane may have been held during the four days between Stan's murder and her own death. Mike turned around in the neighbor's driveway …

… and there at the end of the driveway was a tree with a pronounced lean, the tree from Dean's vision.

Dean Thompson seems to have some "kindred attachment" to Mary Jane, much as Mike Arians does. He has visited the Roadhouse many times, and has grown fond of the young girl's spirit. Much like Mike's experiences, Dean has noticed Mary Jane making herself known to him. He shared a deeply fascinating synchronicity with me.

Dean makes a habit of visiting Mary Jane's grave. When he pays his respects, he leaves two shells on her grave, one facing up, and one facing down. The upwards-facing shell collects fresh rain water to cleanse the spirit, and the shell that faces down is for protection. The first time Dean thought of doing this, he forgot to bring the shells … but something else seemed to be at work.

He shared with me an email he sent to his team: *"I went out to the Roadhouse on Sunday (8/28/2011) … I seem to be pulled toward this place and Sunday was no exception … prior to me leaving I had looked at some shells on my window sill. I thought what a nice thing to bring to the grave of Mary Jane Reed as a symbol or gift. I had walked away from the shells to go look up her gemstone (aquamarine). I looked through [a] collection of gems and did not find any, so I decided the shells would work best.*

"After arriving at the cemetery, I realized I didn't grab the shells ... but to my surprise in front and behind her grave were two shells. One shell was broken (behind the grave) and one was intact. I took the [broken shell] with me ... I will return it I promise ... but I felt that it was a sign to take—who knows, maybe Mary Jane could use the shell to listen to my conversations with Mike."

As Dean told me, "The odds of finding shells by her grave after I had already thought to bring them is a pretty big synchronicity." Add this to the connection Mike Arians feels with Mary Jane, and you've got some interesting questions to ponder.

With all of the investigating that Dean and his team Ghost Head Soup have done at the Roadhouse, they've come up with some intriguing theories about the hauntings there. Dean feels that Mary Jane does not haunt the Roadhouse, but that she watches over the place. (He and others also get the sense that Mary Jane is not an earthbound spirit, but is free.)

Dean also points out that the Roadhouse has a rich history of its own, and is home to different spirits. Besides former owner Esther Stenhouse, one of these may be June "June-Bugg" Arians, Mike's late wife. And given the work and energy Mike has put into researching the Reed-Skridla murder case, there may be another spirit looking over his shoulder ... and that is Willard Burright.

Ghost Head Soup's investigation of the Roadhouse can be found on YouTube.

Love Me Tender (1956)

The 1950s were supposed to have been an idyllic time in America's history. When we think of the post-war years, we think of poodle skirts and sock hops, young couples sharing a shake at a malt shop, Elvis Presley swinging his hips to the new beat of rock and roll. It's thought of as being a safe time, a time when responsible kids could go off to see a movie in the theater, and get home later that evening, having had their fill of popcorn and a double feature.

Sadly, it didn't always turn out that way, even in the 1950s.

The Grimes family lived on Damen Avenue in Chicago. It was a close-knit family, headed by single mother Lorretta. Sisters Patricia and Barbara were especially close. They were both rabid Elvis Presley fans, and they had seen his latest film, *Love Me Tender*, a mind-boggling fourteen times at a theater in Chicago. When they found out that the film was scheduled for a second run at the Brighton Theatre on Archer Avenue, they were ecstatic. The Brighton was much closer to home for them. If they timed it right, they could squeeze in two shows before curfew. Besides, Patricia would be turning thirteen in three days, and seeing the movie again would be a perfect early birthday celebration for the sisters. They made plans to go opening night, December 28, 1956, to see the film for the fifteenth—and final—time.

On the morning of December 28, Barbara got up around 8 am to go to her part-time job in the mailroom of Wolf Furniture House. The behind-the-scenes work suited her—she was timid, nervous even, around strangers. The office manager at the business had tried Barbara in the general office, accepting payments from customers, but it didn't work out. The mailroom was a better fit for the shy fifteen-year-old.

Patricia got up a little later, but was awake to see Barbara before she left for work. The girls made plans to meet for lunch.

After lunch, Barbara went back to work, and Patricia headed home to do chores. When she'd finished, she went for a milkshake with her brothers, Jimmy and Joseph. Then she met a friend at the candy store to buy some comic books. She was home by 4:30, and Barbara came home from work around 6 pm.

The girls rushed through dinner with the family, eager to be off to the theater to swoon over the King. Lorretta was reluctant to let them go. The night was chilly, and Barbara was getting over a cold. But the girls pleaded and cajoled, as teen girls will do, and eventually Lorretta gave in.

The girls left their home at 3634 South Damen around 7:15 in the evening, with $2.50 between them, just enough for bus fare, movie tickets, and snacks. They walked a couple of blocks to the bus stop, and caught the bus straight to the theater.

Patricia's school friend, Dorothy Weinert, sat behind the girls with her own younger sister during the movie. Dorothy and her sister didn't stay for the second half of the double feature, but they did say they saw the Grimes sisters in the popcorn line at the theater during the intermission, around 9:30 pm.

Any information about the girls' whereabouts after that is dubious at best. Many people said they saw the sisters on an eastbound CTA bus around 11 pm, headed into the city, and that they got off the bus at 11:05 at Western Avenue, about halfway to their home. Why they would get off there, instead of closer to home, is unclear. And two teenage boys said they saw the Grimes sisters fooling around near Damen Avenue, "giggling and jumping out of doorways at each other". At that point, around 11:30 at night, they would have been about two blocks from home.

What is known for sure is that Patricia and Barbara were expected home around 11:45 pm. Loretta started to worry when midnight came and went with no sign of the girls. She sent two of her other children, Theresa and Joseph, to the bus stop at 35th and Hoyne, hoping the errant girls would turn up there. Theresa and Joseph waited until 2 am. Three buses came and went, with no sign of Barbara or Patricia. They came home and told their mother the distressing news. At 2:15, Loretta Grimes called the police to report her two daughters missing.

During the next few weeks, the city of Chicago launched one of the largest missing persons investigations ever seen. An unbelievable 300,000 people were questioned. Two thousand of those were interrogated seriously. Acting on a tip that the girls had been seen heading for Nashville, Tennessee, and knowing of their obsession with Elvis, the star himself made an appeal to them on January 19: "If you are good Presley fans, you'll go home and ease your mother's worries."

The theory that the girls had run away from home was considered briefly, then discarded. Loretta Grimes was adamant, as only a mother can be, that her daughters hadn't run away. They had no reason to, she argued. And besides, they had just gotten a much-desired brand-new AM radio for Christmas. Loretta felt sure the girls wouldn't have left such a treasured possession behind.

One of the hundreds of people seriously considered as suspects by the police was Walter Kranz. On January 15, he made an anonymous phone call to the police, claiming that the bodies of the Grimes sisters would be found at a park at 81st and Wolf Road. Furthermore, he claimed that this information had come to him in a dream. Then he hung up. That was enough reason for the police to trace the call. Kranz was picked up for questioning and held at the Englewood police station for some time. He was given multiple lie detector tests, but was later released when the police could find no solid evidence linking him to the murders.

Another suspect was seventeen-year-old Max Fleig. He was brought in to be questioned, and offered to take a lie detector test, which he failed. In the middle of the test, he confessed to kidnapping the girls. However, at that time, it was illegal to perform a lie detector test on a minor. The test was inadmissible, despite Fleig having taken it voluntarily. The police had to let him go free. Fleig was sent to prison a few years later for the brutal murder of a young woman.

The frantic search for the Grimes sisters came to a tragic end on January 22, 1957. Leonard Prescott, a construction worker, was driving south on German Church Road near Willow Springs when he happened to glance at the side of the road. Just past the guard rail, he thought he saw the white, tangled limbs of two discarded clothing mannequins. That was just weird enough for him to stop and take a second look. He went and got his wife, Marie, and cautiously they went up to the guard rail and peered over.

The waxy limbs didn't belong to mannequins. The nude bodies of Patricia and Barbara Grimes had been tossed at the side of the road. Whoever did the body dump wasn't even concerned enough with being caught to kick the bodies over the dropoff into the ravine and Devil's Creek, just a few feet beyond. Marie Prescott was so upset at the sight of the bodies that she fainted and had to be carried back to the car.

The bodies could be mistaken for dummies—they weren't arranged in any meaningful way. They had simply been dumped at the side of the road. Barbara lay face down, on her left side, with her knees slightly drawn up. Patricia lay face up, her body carelessly thrown on top of Barbara's. Both girls had wounds and bruises that remain unexplained to this day.

The first working theory, put forth by Cook County Sheriff Joseph D. Lohman and Harry Glos, an investigator for the coroner's office, was that the girls had been dumped there just after their deaths, which they estimated as being around January 9. There had been a heavy snowfall that day, with temperatures falling enough to preserve the bodies as they looked at the time of death. Besides, the bodies were so close to the road, it was difficult to imagine they hadn't been seen between December 28 and January 9, when there would have been no snow to cover them.

Furthermore, the officials pointed to a thin layer of ice that encased the bodies. That could only have been formed, the investigators theorized, as snow fell and melted on the cooling bodies. It takes time for a corpse to lose its body heat. Even a body that had been dead for a few hours would retain enough heat to melt falling snowflakes for a while, allowing a scrim of ice to form as the water froze.

But the autopsies told a different story. When the bodies had thawed, the coroners at the Cook County Morgue examined the girls' stomach contents. They discovered that the last food the girls had eaten was the popcorn at the show. According to this, the girls had to have been killed within hours of their kidnapping on December 28.

So which physical evidence should we believe? The ice on the bodies? Or the stomach contents? The physical evidence actually contradicts itself, which should not be possible.

The investigators were equally baffled. Three experienced pathologists performed the autopsies. Although the official cause of death was "murder", the best they could do as far as explanation was "secondary shock due to exposure to the elements". And they only wrote that down because they couldn't determine any other cause of death. Meaning, oddly enough, that none of the wounds on the girls' bodies were fatal ones.

Patricia and Barbara were buried on January 28, 1957, one month after they went missing. Portrait photos of the girls were propped on their white caskets. They were buried in Holy Sepulchre Catholic Cemetery.

But the Grimes sisters may not rest in peace. German Church Road is the site of a residual haunting. Many witnesses have reported hearing a car pull off to the side of the road at the dump site. There is the squeaking crunch of a car door opening, then two sickening thumps—dead meat hitting frozen ground. The door slams shut, the engine revs, and the car pulls away. All of this is heard, never seen. But the Grimes sisters are not forgotten.

The Woods Are Lonely, Dark, and Deep (late 1970s)

There are pockets of weirdness scattered around this big old world of ours, places steeped in mystery, where the rational day-to-day business of the 21st century gets really fuzzy around the edges.

One of these places is the Bridgewater Triangle, an area of about 200 square miles tucked into southeastern Massachusetts. If it's weird, it's here: Satanic cults, a threatening phantom hitchhiker, Native American curses, UFO sightings going as far back as 1760, mysterious cryptids known as pukwudgies, Hockamock Swamp, known by the Wampanoag as "the place where spirits dwell", and the Assonet Ledge in Freetown State Forest, where visitors report seeing ghosts jumping from the ledge to their apparent doom ... and often feel a compulsion themselves to hurtle off the cliff.

The Freetown State Forest was the scene of a real-life nightmare in the late 1970s. On the afternoon of September 8, 1978, 15-year-old Mary Lou Arruda disappeared from nearby Raynham. A newspaper delivery boy found her bicycle near the scene, but nothing more turned up ...

... until two months later, in November, when Arruda's decomposed body was discovered tied to a tree in the forest. According to the coroner's report, Arruda had been tied to the tree in a standing position—and had been alive when it happened. When she lost consciousness, the weight of her head against the rope around her neck caused her to suffocate.

James M. Kater, a doughnut maker from Brockton, was

indicted for Arruda's murder. His car had been spotted in Raynham, and the vehicle was marred by a nine-inch gash that matched Arruda's bike. Kater, 32 years old at the time of Arruda's murder, was also on probation for kidnapping a girl in Andover in 1968. Kater stood trial four times, and his final appeal was rejected by the US Supreme Court in 2007. Kater died, still incarcerated, on January 9, 2016.

Kater's arrest and conviction for the murder of Mary Lou Arruda may have kept him from turning into a serial killer. A newspaper article announcing his death described Kater as "evil encased in a human body."

The location where Arruda's body was found is jumping with paranormal activity. Paranormal investigators have written in to the *Unexplained Mysteries* forum to tell of their experiences. One source wrote of the negative energy that permeates the forest. "I had the distinct feeling that we were being followed and watched," he wrote.

Another investigator made similar claims. "I have seen the spirit of a girl near the site where they found Mary Lou Arruda's body in 1978. I recently spent the entire night in the forest with my group. We had some people feel like they were pushed. We heard laughter in the woods. Occasionally, we heard groans, breathing, and screams." The witness also reported seeing softball-sized ghost lights flickering in the tops of the trees.

Arruda's murder was not the only violence to stain Freetown State Forest. Karen Marsden, a woman believed to be a prostitute in Fall River, was brutally killed in February 1980. The 20-year-old had been picked up by the police on February 8. The police wanted information from her. She was being interviewed as a possible witness to the October 1979 killing of another Fall River prostitute, Doreen Levesque. The cops liked a guy named Carl Drew for the murder. Levesque had been found October 13, 1979, under the bleachers at Diman Vocational High School. Her head and face had been crushed with a rock, and she'd been tied up with fishing line. She'd also been abused with a baseball bat.

The cops had heard rumors about Satanic rituals being performed in the forest, and they wanted Marsden to take them to the sites of these rituals. But Marsden refused to cooperate; she was sobbing, and panicked to the point of incoherence. She begged the police to drop her off at St. Mary's church, so she could visit the priest. The police did as Marsden asked.

Marsden had very little time to live after that meeting with the cops. Two months later, in April, investigators found part of her skull and a few clumps of hair in the forest. That's all they ever found.

Carl Drew was eventually accused of instigating three cult-like murders, those of Levesque, Marsden, and Barbara Raposa. The "son of Satan", as he was called, was a self-proclaimed devil worshipper who led Satanic gatherings in the forest—gatherings that sometimes ended in murder.

Robin Murphy, one of Drew's sex workers and a wanna-be pimp, testified against Carl Drew and another man, Andrew Maltais. She said that she, Drew, and two others had driven Karen Marsden to the woods. They'd gotten out of the car, and Murphy began to drag Marsden through the woods by her hair. Drew told Marsden to give Murphy a ring she was wearing, but she refused. Drew cut her finger off, and gave Murphy the ring.

Murphy, who claimed to have been possessed by Satan, said that when Drew demanded she slit Marsden's throat, she did it. Then she tore Marsden's head off and kicked it. Drew then mutilated Marsden's body, carving an X on her chest. He dipped his fingers in the murdered woman's blood, and marked an X on Murphy's forehead while speaking in what Murphy called a demonic tongue. He told her that with the bloody anointing, she'd been initiated into his cult. "The killing of Doreen Levesque was an offering of the soul to Satan and so was the killing of Miss Marsden," Murphy told the court. She claimed that the skulls of the victims were used in Black Mass rituals in the Freetown State Forest.

Murphy's testimony helped convict Maltais (who died while incarcerated) and Drew (who is still in prison for the murders). However, Robin Murphy did not get off scot-free in return for her testimony. For her part in the vicious killings, she was convicted of second-degree murder and sentenced to life in prison.

Seventeen years old at the time of the murders, Robin had little schooling, but her IQ was north of 137. Smart and precocious, she practiced paganism before she was ten years old. She fell in with a bad crowd very early in life; Andrew Maltais was a pedophile who had been preying on Murphy since she was eleven years old. Even though she claimed that she didn't participate in Marsden's murder, she was still denied parole after several hearings. At the March 2017 parole hearing, Representative Alan Silvia said, "Robin was the mastermind in all three homicides and manipulated everyone."

The Fall River Cult Murders case inspired a flurry of Black Mass activity in Freetown State Forest during the Satanic Panic of the 1980s. One man, William LaFrance, was discovered camping in the forest surrounded by lit candles and Satanic symbols drawn in the dirt. Park rangers also found freshly painted skulls, pentagrams, and other occult graffiti at haunted Assonet Ledge.

So is Freetown State Forest haunted because of the murders? Or were killers drawn to the woods because of some malevolent energy?

The thorny chicken-and-egg question has its origins in the history of the area. Freetown was purchased in 1659 from the Wampanoag tribe—or more precisely, from Wamsutta, the sachem of the Wampanoag. Wamsutta was the oldest son of Massasoit, who formed an alliance with the settlers of Plymouth and saved them from starving during the early years in the New World.

Wamsutta really couldn't catch a break. He sold land that his people considered highly sacred, and he might not have had the support of his tribe in the sale. Then, the English accused him of making an alliance with the Narragansett tribe, which was unfriendly to the settlers. The English marched Wamsutta at musket point to Plymouth, where he died of a "sudden illness"—which the Wampanoag and other tribes took to mean that he had been poisoned by the English.

Wamsutta's sale of his ancestral lands didn't sit well with the Wampanoag, a feeling that has persisted to this day. The Wampanoag believe that the savage murders in the forest have affected the spirits that dwell there. They feel that the murders and cult activity have turned the once-gentle forest spirits violent. This attracts evil to the forest, and the forest is in turn fed by that evil. Native Americans feel that the hauntings and the crimes won't stop until the land is returned to the Wampanoag tribe.

However the souring of the Freetown State Forest happened, it is inarguably a place of palpable, almost electric intensity. Rachel Hoffman from Paranormal Xpeditions produced a documentary on Freetown in 2014. She said that the serene forest turned nightmarish after dark. The seasoned ghost hunter believes that the Freetown State Forest is "a hotbed of primordial evil."

Paranormal author Sam Baltrusis has wandered in the forest as well. He says, "Is it haunted? Absolutely. It's as if the Freetown State Forest has a devilish mind of its own." Baltrusis visited the forest with demonologist James Annitto. They drove past the site on Copicut Road where Mary Lou Arruda was tied to a tree and left to die. The whole area had, as Baltrusis says, "an inexplicable energy that was unsettling to me. Something didn't feel right."

His apprehension was soon racheted up several notches. As he and Annitto started to walk down Upper Ledge Road, headed towards Freetown Ledge (another paranormal hot spot), they were attacked by a swarm of locust-like insects. Annitto, the demonologist and a deacon in the Catholic Church, later told Baltrusis that locusts are a symbol of God's wrath. He felt that perhaps it was a sign that the men were trespassing where they weren't meant to go. He did assure me that it was an interesting experience, one he's not likely to forget.

The Day the Music Died (1980)

The young, pudgy man in the aviator glasses paced the sidewalk in front of the hotel. He clutched a book, worrying and bending its red cover in his hands. The kid was a big Beatles fan, and he was in front of the Dakota Hotel in New York City. He'd come all the way from Hawaii to meet rock star John Lennon. He blended in with the others; it wasn't unusual for knots of Lennon's fans to cluster around the entrance to the Dakota, all of them hoping to catch a glimpse of their idol, or better yet, have a short chat with him as he signed an autograph.

The kid was distracted, chatting with the other fans who'd gathered for a glimpse of their idol, so he missed seeing Lennon step out of a cab and walk into the hotel. Lennon went up to his apartment on the seventh floor, right across the hall from Roberta Flack. He and his wife Yoko Ono were hosting the famous portrait photographer Annie Leibowitz.

Leibowitz was there to do a photo shoot for *Rolling Stone* magazine. She took several photos of John, and suggested that a photo of the two musicians naked would make a daring cover for the magazine. In fact, she *promised* it would be the cover. Originally, the plan was that one of her photos of John would be the picture used for the cover. John, ever loyal to his wife, insisted that Yoko be on the cover too, but she demurred at nudity for the shot. Leibowitz compromised, and artfully arranged a photo—a (butt-naked) John curled against a (fully-clothed) Yoko.

After the photo shoot, John did a radio interview, then he and Yoko left for the Record Plant to work on mixing "Walking On Thin Ice", a song written by Yoko that featured John on lead guitar.

John and Yoko left their apartment at 5 pm and headed down to the limousine that would take them to the studio. As they came out of the building, the bespectacled young man approached them, clutching John's album *Double Fantasy*, asking for the musician's autograph. This was, of course, an everyday occurrence for John Lennon, former Beatle and famous guitarist. He was known for treating fans with courtesy and grace, especially fans who had been waiting for hours to see him.

Another Lennon fan, Paul Goresh, snapped a picture of Lennon signing the young man's album. The young man himself later recalled his encounter with the famous rock star. "He was very kind to me. Ironically, very kind and was very patient with me. The limousine was waiting ... and he took his time with me and he got the pen going and he signed my album. He asked me if I needed anything else. I said, 'No. No sir.' And he walked away. Very cordial and decent man."

Which made what happened later that night even more inexplicable.

John and Yoko spent several hours at the studio working on Yoko's song. They returned to the Dakota around 10:50 that night. John wanted to say goodnight to their son Sean, then he and Yoko planned to go out to the Stage Deli restaurant. Instead of driving into the courtyard of the Dakota, the limo let John and Yoko off on 72nd Street in front of the arched entrance of the hotel. The couple got out, John carrying the tape of the final mix of "Walking On Thin Ice".

The young man, who was still waiting on the sidewalk in front of the hotel, nodded at Yoko as she passed him. John gave the kid a brief glance, as if he recognized him from earlier that evening.

Then Mark David Chapman reached inside his coat pocket, pulled out a Charter Arms .38 Special revolver, and emptied all five shots into John Lennon from nine or ten feet away. One shot went wide and hit a hotel window. But the other four hollow-point rounds tore into Lennon's body—two in his left shoulder, and two in his back, where they ripped through his left lung and destroyed vital arteries around his heart.

Lennon, blood pouring from his wounds, staggered into

the reception area of the hotel. More blood sprayed from his mouth as he gurgled, "I'm shot! I'm shot!" He collapsed, and the cassette tape in his hand spun and skittered across the floor.

The doorman, Jose Perdomo, grabbed Chapman and shook the gun from his hand, then kicked it, sending it spinning across the pavement. "Do you know what you just did?" he shouted.

Chapman replied with eerie calm, "I just shot John Lennon." He pulled a book out of his coat pocket and opened it, lowered his gaze, and began to read.

Mark David Chapman *was* a Beatles fan. He was also one strange puppy. Twenty-five years old at the time of the shooting, he lived in Hawaii and worked as a security guard. He had no criminal history before the one violent act with which he upended the world. Chapman was obsessed with J. D. Salinger's novel *The Catcher in the Rye,* and really identified with the novel's protagonist, Holden Caulfield. One of the book's main themes, beloved of high school English teachers everywhere, is Caulfield's rage against adult hypocrisy.

Since Chapman was a Beatles fan, it must have torn him up inside when, in 1966, John Lennon claimed that the Beatles were "more popular than Jesus." Chapman also took umbrage with the lyrics to Lennon's song "God", from his first post-Beatles solo album. Lennon used the lyrics to lay out a list of things he doesn't believe in, including God, Buddha, Jesus, Hitler, Kennedy, kings, the Bible, tarot, (rather confoundingly) Bob Dylan, and (heartbreakingly) the Beatles. He sings that he only believes in himself and in Yoko. He describes God as "a concept by which we measure our pain." Lennon later explained, "If there is a God, we're all it."

But what rankled Chapman the most, given his passion for emulating Holden Caulfield, was what he saw as Lennon's hypocrisy. In the song "Imagine", Lennon the artist sings "imagine no possessions", but Lennon the rock star had possessions—lots and lots and lots of them. Chapman had assumed that after the breakup of the Beatles, Lennon was living a relatively simple life in retirement at Tittenhurst Park. (This was John and Yoko's 72-acre country home from the late summer of 1969 to August 1971. Fun fact number one: Ringo Starr also lived there with his family, from 1973 into the late 1980s.) Instead, Lennon had returned to his musical career, and moved to New York City, taking an apartment in the Dakota Hotel, living the lavish lifestyle of a rock star. And John and Yoko didn't own just one apartment in the Dakota—they owned five.

Chapman bought a five-shot .38 caliber revolver in Honolulu for $169. He did his research—he contacted the FAA to find out how he could transport the weapon legally. On the flight, he listened to the music he'd brought with him. He had recorded fourteen hours of Beatles music to listen to on the plane from Hawaii and while he was wandering around New York City. His favorite parts of the mix tape were the tracks he'd added. Over some of the songs, he'd added a track of himself screaming "John Lennon must die!" and "John Lennon is a phony!"

Concierge attendant Jay Hastings ripped open John's blood-drenched shirt as the musician lay gasping for air through a ruined lung. On seeing the multiple gunshot wounds, Hastings realized that Lennon needed far more help than he could provide at that moment. He covered John's chest with his own uniform jacket, removed the musician's round glasses—now spattered with blood—and called the police.

Officers Peter Cullen and Steven Spiro arrived two minutes later; they'd been just a few blocks away, at 72nd Street and Broadway, when they heard a report of shots fired at the Dakota. When they arrived, they found a surreal scene—one of the most famous musicians in the world bleeding out on the floor of a hotel lobby, and his assassin standing on the sidewalk outside that same hotel, calmly reading a paperback copy of *The Catcher in the Rye*. Chapman made no attempt to resist as the officers whapped handcuffs on him and shoved him into the back of their squad car. He even apologized meekly for having ruined their night. Cullen snarled, incredulous, "You've got to be fucking kidding me. You're worried about our night? Do you know what you just did to your *life*?"

More police officers arrived and hustled into the Dakota, where they found John lying face down on the floor of the reception area, blood pouring from his mouth and soaking his clothes. Hastings hovered nearby, trying his best to help the dying man. Officers Herb Frauenberger and Tony Palma were soon joined by two more cops, Bill Gamble and James Moran. Frauenberger bundled Lennon into Gamble and Moran's squad car, and they drove him to Roosevelt Hospital. On the way there, John tried to speak, but could only manage a gurgling moan. Soon, he lost consciousness.

The police car pulled up at the hospital a few minutes before 11 pm. Less than ten minutes had passed since four rounds had ripped into John Lennon's body. But even with the cops' swift response, John was already gone. When Officer Moran staggered into the emergency room with Lennon on his back and tipped him onto a gurney, Lennon wasn't breathing, and had no pulse.

Half a dozen medical professionals worked on Lennon, trying in vain to resuscitate him. In a last-ditch effort to get him back, the doctors cut his chest open to try a Hail Mary open heart massage to get some circulation going. But when they looked at the damage, they knew all hope was gone. One bullet had lodged in Lennon's aorta, right beside his heart. And other major arteries were shredded with the passage of the hollow-point rounds. The coroner later reported that no one could have survived for more than a few minutes with that much internal damage. John was pronounced dead on arrival. In an eerie coincidence, at the moment he was pronounced, witnesses heard the Beatles' song "All My Loving" playing over the hospital's piped-in sound system.

Yoko asked the hospital not to report John's death to the media right away, and she had a very good reason for the request. John and Yoko's five-year-old son Sean was still up, and probably watching TV, Yoko said. She wanted to tell Sean of John's death herself, before he saw it splashed all over the television.

The news was leaked by a TV producer, Alan Weiss, who happened to be waiting for treatment in the emergency room of Roosevelt Hospital. He'd been in a motorcycle accident in Central Park about an hour before, and was still waiting to be seen when the police rushed Lennon in. Weiss's ears were ringing from the accident, and at first he didn't trust his hearing when he overheard people talking about the tragic shooting. After confirming the news, Weiss called his station and told them what was going on.

The news of John Lennon's death broke during the last few moments of the Monday Night Football broadcast. The New England Patriots and the Miami Dolphins were battling on the gridiron, and the game was tied, with the Patriots hoping to pull off a field goal to win the game. ABC News' president, Roone Arledge, told Frank Gifford and Howard Cosell about the shooting, and asked them to break into the game with the news. Cosell drew the short straw, but balked at being the bearer of such tidings. Cosell had interviewed John Lennon in 1974 (during Monday Night Football, eerily enough), and was stunned at the news. Gifford convinced Cosell to deliver the message. "You've got to," he told his colleague. "If you know it, we've got to do it. Don't hang on it. It's a tragic moment, and this is going to shake up the whole world."

The two newsmen, both consummate professionals, returned to their reporting, but their audience could sense the foreboding in their voices. Gifford continued to call the plays, but added, "Timeout is called with three seconds remaining ... I don't care what's on the line, Howard, you have got to say what we know in the booth."

Cosell replied, "Yes, we have to say it. Remember this is just a football game, no matter who wins or loses." Then he went on to report the "unspeakable tragedy" of John Lennon's death to a stunned and grieving world. Rock stations all over the country immediately switched to playing Lennon's music.

John Lennon was cremated the day after he died. His ashes were scattered in Central Park, within sight of his and Yoko's apartment. (In 1985, New York City would dedicate an area of Central Park directly across from the Dakota as a memorial site for the fallen musician, calling it Strawberry Fields. This was an area where John loved to take walks, drinking in the natural beauty of Central Park, an oasis in the middle of the bustling city.)

Yoko Ono decided not to hold a funeral for John. In the statement she released to the press, she said, "Later in the week we will set the time for a silent vigil to pray for his soul. We invite you to participate from wherever you are at the time ... John loved and prayed for the human race. Please pray the same for him. Love, Yoko and Sean."

For those ten minutes, every radio station in New York City went off the air.

John Lennon's death reverberated around the world. Annie Leibowitz's photograph, with a nude John curled around a sweetly tolerant Yoko, did indeed appear on the cover of *Rolling Stone*, for their January 22, 1981 memorial issue. The photographer's promise did come true—just not in the way that any of them expected. (Fun fact number two: in 2005, the American Society of Magazine Editors ranked it as the top magazine cover of the last forty years.)

At least three Beatles fans committed suicide in the days after John's death. A distraught Yoko pleaded with fans not to harm themselves—it wasn't what John would have wanted. But as his widow, she made her own feelings clear. Yoko released a solo album, *Season of Glass*, in 1981. The album cover was a picture of John's round wire-rimmed glasses, spattered with his own blood.

George Harrison issued a public statement of his own about his friend's death. Privately, he mourned to friends, "I just wanted to be in a band. Here we are, twenty years later, and some whack job has shot my mate. I just wanted to play guitar in a band."

John Lennon is not forgotten. For years, Yoko put a lit candle in the window of Lennon's room at the Dakota every year on December 8th. It's a sweet gesture of remembrance, a signal to a lost soul to guide him home.

And it seems to have worked.

The first reported sighting of Lennon's ghost was in 1983, when Amanda Moores and musician Joey Harrow saw Lennon standing in the archway at the Dakota's entrance, mere yards from where he'd been gunned down. Perhaps being so close to the scene of his murder had put Lennon in a pensive, even foul mood. Moores almost walked up to the Beatle to say hello, but she said the look on his face let her know he wasn't in the mood to chat with strangers.

Lennon was in a much better frame of mind when he showed up in his own apartment. Yoko Ono lived at the Dakota for twenty years after her husband's death. One day she came into the living room to see John's ghost sitting at his white piano. He turned to her and said, "Don't be afraid. I am still with you." Then he vanished.

(Fun fact number three: before his death, Lennon claimed to have had his own paranormal experiences in the Dakota. He told of seeing a phantom he called the Crying Lady, who would pace the Dakota's hallways. Lennon was not alone. Many other witnesses have reported seeing the Crying Lady. She may be the spirit of Elise Vesley, who was manager of the building through the 1930s, '40s, and '50s. Vesley herself, in life, believed passionately in the paranormal. She even claimed to have telekinetic powers. Unfortunately, her son was hit and killed by a truck outside the Dakota. In response to the tragedy, Elise became very protective of the children in the hotel. This sense of responsibility may be why she still haunts the halls of the building.)

Philip Michael, a maintenance man at the Dakota, had a strange experience the night of the murder. John had just been shot, and all hell was breaking loose. Michael went out to the entryway of the hotel. An object caught his eye as it fell to the sidewalk from a decorative flower urn sculpted into the entryway. It was an autographed copy of *Double Fantasy*. Michael propped it back in the urn, thinking "this belongs to someone." It fell out again. No matter how many times he put it there, it kept toppling out. Finally, he took it for safekeeping. Later, he learned that the police were looking for it, so he handed it over. After the trial, he filled out paperwork to get it back. The album cover was quite the worse for wear; investigators had dusted it for prints, and there were Chapman's fingerprints immortalized in gray on the white cardboard. Michael realized that he had the last autograph John Lennon ever signed.

Several years after the murder, in April 1987, the magazine *Fate* ran an article about the strange experiences people had after Lennon's death. One woman described her encounter with Lennon's spirit the day after the shooting. She had stacked several sets of records against a wall in the living room, like you do. Each set of records was seven or eight inches thick, standing on end and leaning against the wall, with the stacks of albums side by side.

The author was thinking of John's senseless death, and trying to take some comfort in the idea that life goes on. She wondered where John was at that moment, the day after his death. If he could communicate with those left behind, what would he say? Did he have an important message to get across? The woman closed her eyes and concentrated on John, mentally saying, "If you're here, and there's something you want to say about what happened to you, or any other message, please know that I am listening."

A noise from the corner of the room made her open her eyes. Looking around for the source of the noise, she realized that one of the stacks of records was falling forward, one by one, very slowly. It looked as if someone invisible was flipping through them. The woman wrote that none of the stacks of albums had ever fallen before. She could see the titles on each album as they fell ... then they stopped falling. The woman gasped—the records had stopped at the only Beatles album in the stack.

From across the room, she could see the album cover. She saw the four Beatles in the picture, and from the cover, John seemed to be looking straight at her. She stared back in disbelief, taking in the whole tableau. Then she realized with a start that right there in front of her was the answer to the question she had asked, the personal message she had wanted from John Lennon. It was the title of the album: she heard it as if the words had been spoken aloud ... LET IT BE.

Murder in Golden Gate Park (1981)

Golden Gate Park, in San Francisco, is not the kind of place you'd want to go camping. But Leroy Carter, Jr., had no choice. The 29-year-old African American had survived the Vietnam War, but things hadn't gone his way when he returned to civilian life. He had ended up homeless, a petty criminal, just another casualty of the war. On February 8, 1981, Carter unrolled his sleeping bag next to Alvord Lake, crawled into it … and never came out.

When police arrived at the scene the next morning, they discovered a headless corpse rolled up in a sleeping bag. Fingerprints told investigators Leroy Carter Jr.'s identity, but they couldn't tell the police why Carter's head was missing. Or why there was a headless chicken about fifty yards away. Or why Carter had two kernels of corn and a chicken wing jammed into the stump of his neck where his head had been the day before.

The police department assigned Officer Sandi Gallant to the case. Gallant had worked on the recent Jonestown Massacre, and had become the SFPD's resident expert on cults, Satanic murders, and religious ritualistic killings. With help from Charles Wetli, the coroner in Dade County, Florida, Gallant came up with a theory.

Both Gallant and Wetli were convinced that the murder had something to do with the dark rituals of Palo Mayombe, an offshoot of Santeria that focused on black magic. According to Gallant's research, Carter's head had been taken for use in a ritual that called for human body parts—the brain, and maybe the ears and nose too. The potion would be finished in 42 days, and to complete the ritual, the head would have to be returned to the scene of the murder.

It was a solid theory, but no one was convinced … not even Gallant. On March 22, the 42nd day after the murder, none of the police were at the park. Gallant had second-guessed herself, and she and her partner decided not to set up a stakeout. The killer completed the ritual, placing Carter's head in the weeds near Alvord Lake.

The head revealed no new clues, and the case went cold. Leroy Carter Jr. was buried in Arlington National Cemetery in Virginia. His murder remains unsolved.

Murder in Plymouth (1996)

About halfway between Plymouth Rock and Burial Hill in Plymouth, Massachusetts, is a pleasant little road called Leyden Street. It wasn't always called this; it started out as First Street, and for a very good reason. This is the ... well, the first street laid out by the Pilgrims, before Christmas in 1620, the year they landed on these shores. In 1823, it was renamed Leyden Street, in honor of the city in Holland where the Pilgrims paused for a while before coming to the New World. It claims to be the oldest continuously inhabited street in the thirteen colonies.

At 21 Leyden Street there stands an apartment building. It looks perfectly ordinary, just like the others on the street, a pretty, neat example of architecture that even the Pilgrims would have admired. But there is something that sets this dwelling well apart from the other tidy New England buildings on this little slice of Plymouth. In 1997, police made a truly horrifying discovery in the attic of 21 Leyden Street.

But let's turn the clock back a bit. In 1996, a married couple, Victor and Carol Ann Cardarelli, lived in a third-floor apartment in the building. The relationship was fraught, to say the least. Although they both worked, the Cardarellis were having financial issues. In late 1996, Victor was trying to settle some child support obligations (he had children from a previous marriage). In order to facilitate this, he gave up his claim to a share of a house he owned with his ex-wife. This frustrated Carol deeply; she had been hoping that she and Victor could buy a house of their own, and move out of the apartment.

To add to the precariousness of their financial situation, less than three weeks later, Victor lost his job. Carol's friends and relatives couldn't help but notice her anxiety, heightened by these two blows to their stability. In fact, Carol was feeling quite overwhelmed.

In early November, Carol missed a friend's wedding. And after the Veteran's Day weekend, she didn't return to work. Coworkers and relatives alike had questions—lots of them. But Victor had answers for them ... sort of.

On November 11, 1996, when a coworker called the apartment to check up on Carol's tardiness—she was usually on time—Victor told her that Carol had gone to California. He said that a member of Carol's family had been in a serious car accident.

But when Linda Hendrick, Carol's daughter-in-law, called too, Victor told a different tale. He said that Carol was in the hospital recovering from dental work. Linda, doing her own sleuthing, called all the hospitals in the Plymouth area. Unsurprisingly, her search turned up no clue as to Carol's whereabouts. Suspicious and worried, Linda called the police.

The Plymouth police had also been contacted by one of Carol's coworkers, so on November 17, they took a quick look inside the apartment. They found it immaculate ... but empty. Carol and Victor were both gone. Linda stayed in contact with the police throughout December 1996 and early January 1997, but the police didn't have any leads.

They did, however, have an idea that something hinky was going on. Detective John Rogers Jr. of the Plymouth police department put together a paper trail on Victor Cardarelli. Following this trail revealed that Victor had taken out numerous credit card advances, and had drained his bank accounts (held jointly with Carol). Then he'd gambled the money at various casinos in Connecticut and Atlantic City, New Jersey between November 9—a day after Carol was last seen—and November 24.

Victor spent two weeks living it up in Atlantic City. He made two cash withdrawals from his and Carol's joint bank account totaling $5,000, which left a zero balance. He bought $7,500 worth of traveler's checks, nearly wiping out another joint account. He made at least seven cash advances on credit cards at various casinos, totaling nearly $11,000. And to add insult to injury, he pawned Carol's gold necklace—for $35.

He had a story ready for this part of his adventure too—a sob story. He told a casino employee that his wife had died of cancer, and that his coworkers had generously taken up a collection so that he could travel to Atlantic City.

After his gambling spree in New Jersey, Victor spent eleven weeks racking up miles on the lam. He drove to Key West, Florida, and visited his mother at her mobile home park in Barefoot Bay. He told her yet another story. He got as far as telling her that Carol was dying ... when his mother told *him* that the police were looking for him.

Carol's friends and relatives, including Linda Hendrick, were still leaning on the police to solve the mystery of her sudden disappearance. The nationally broadcast true crime show *America's Most Wanted* even got involved.

Victor realized the heat was on. He left his mother's home within hours, and spent several weeks driving around the southern US. He wandered as far as Galveston, Texas, living in his car, eating at fast food joints, and bathing at rest stops or in hotel swimming pools. In February 1997, he made his way back north to Atlantic City.

Meanwhile, the landlord of Victor and Carol's apartment told Linda that the Cardarellis were so far behind on their rent, he was planning to evict them. Carol was still missing, and Victor, too, was nowhere to be found. So Linda and her husband decided to clean out the apartment.

They arrived in Plymouth January 10, 1997. When they stepped into the apartment, they noticed an odd smell—a pungent odor that stung Linda's nose, almost like vinegar. They also noticed, as they made their way through the place, that some of Carol's clothes and jewelry were missing. Linda's uneasy feeling led her and her husband into the couple's bedroom. They turned the mattress over, and discovered bloodstains and bloody towels. Horrified, they immediately contacted the authorities.

State troopers found three blood-stained towels on the box spring mattress. The mattress itself was liberally soaked with blood, and there was castoff blood spatter on the walls and ceiling of the bedroom. This was enough for the police to bring in a cadaver dog to search for a body.

The next day, Saturday, January 11, the dog led police to the attic of the apartment building. A body, tightly wrapped in bedding and plastic, was found in a crawl space behind a wall in the attic. Dental records proved that the partially decomposed corpse was Carol Ann Cardarelli. She had been missing for over three months.

An autopsy revealed that Carol had died in early November, and that she had suffered numerous fractures of her face and skull and severe damage to her brain. The official cause of death was severe blunt force trauma to the head. Semicircular fractures in her skull matched a cast iron frying pan that was found near the bed. Blood spatter analysis showed that she had been struck at least three times, possibly more.

By Sunday afternoon, Victor Cardarelli was wanted for murder.

The discovery of Carol's body was a shock to the community. It was made even worse by the fact that searchers had already looked in the attic the month before her body was actually found. Diane Knight lived across the hall from the Cardarellis. She and one of Carol's sons had searched the attic without success. Knight told a reporter from Plymouth's *Old Colony Memorial* newspaper that she had even looked into the crawl space where Carol's body was hidden, but personal belongings were blocking her view into the small space, and she was reluctant to go poking through them. "I was within inches," she said later.

Diane and Carol's son decided instead to look in a different part of the attic. The newspaper account said that according to local legend, the other hideaway had been used as part of the Underground Railroad. Even as she helped look for her friend, Diane hoped that Carol would soon turn up safe and sound. Those hopes were dashed when Carol's body was discovered under the front eaves of the building, just above Diane's second-floor apartment.

"I'm in shock," Diane told reporter Rich Harbert. "It's still just starting to sink in that I lived there for two months with her up in the attic like that." (Diane had moved out of the building just a week before the gruesome discovery.) "She didn't deserve to be chucked in a corner like that. She was a really nice person. She didn't deserve what she got."

Diane wasn't alone in her shock and grief. Carol was described by all as "an elegant lady", "a wonderful, kind, and caring person." All of Plymouth was horrified that such a violent crime could claim such a lovely lady—and on one of the most historic streets in America, no less. But now that the victim had been found, the hunt was on for her murderer.

Since Victor Cardarelli was known to be a gambler, and since he'd hung out for a while in Atlantic City right after Carol had disappeared, authorities focused their search there. The town was plastered with fliers describing him. On February 4, 1997, Victor used his casino loyalty reward card to try and cash out what was left in his account—a whopping $236. A sharp-eyed cashier recognized him and called the police. He was arrested at the Resorts Casino Hotel in Atlantic City. He told law enforcement officers that he intended to win enough money to pay off his bills, then he was going to turn himself in. (Yeah, right, uh-huh.)

Victor was taken back to Massachusetts. He told detectives that he remembered Carol bleeding from the face, but that he couldn't remember how or why he had killed her. He did, though, admit to wrapping her corpse in bedding, then in plastic, and hiding it in the attic.

During the murder trial, the Commonwealth showed the jury autopsy photos during the medical examiner's testimony. This is never a fun thing for anyone, but the prosecution tried to go about it as tactfully and tastefully as possible. The pictures were cropped to show just the fatal wounds, not decomposing flesh. Victor was upset about this, but he'd really brought it on himself; since he claimed not to remember how he killed Carol, the prosecution had to use the photos to prove that the murder was a case of extreme violence and atrocity. The pictures graphically illustrated the nature and the extent of the fatal injuries in a way that the medical examiner's spoken testimony could not. Victor Cardarelli was convicted of first-degree murder.

Five years later, in March 2001, Victor appeared in court again. He claimed that the Commonwealth's use of autopsy photos influenced the jury, and that he didn't get a fair trial. He also thought it was unfair that the prosecution told the jury about his gambling spree after the murder and his wanderings through the South. He argued that his travels in plain sight in populated areas, and his extensive use of credit cards, meant that he didn't attempt to avoid arrest.

The Supreme Court disagreed. "We have examined the photographs and conclude that they are not unnecessarily gruesome or shocking," was the response. "If photographs of a victim have evidentiary value, as these undeniably do, their gruesome nature does not render them inadmissable." In addition, during the original trial, the judge looked at each picture and (thoughtfully) warned the jurors that the images might be distressing. The conviction of murder in the first degree stood.

The grisly business of Carol Ann Cardarelli's murder was not restricted to autopsy photos shown to a forewarned jury. After police had investigated the apartment and the crime scene had been released, movers came in to clean out the place. During the cleanout, they left the box spring propped against the dumpster, planning to take it to the dump with the next load. When they returned for it, though, it was gone. Someone had taken it. As far as anyone knows, that mattress is still out there somewhere.

The apartment in the building at 21 Leyden Street still holds a vague imprint of Carol's spirit. Ghost tours in the area mention the apartment as a haunted site, although it is not open for investigation. But tour guides who paid attention noticed that for a very long time, no tenants stayed in the apartment for more than a few months.

An interesting story from the apartment gives a hint about the haunting, even if most tenants don't talk about their experiences. According to local stories, Carol was a huge fan of the 1970s television program *Little House on the Prairie*. Tenants have admitted that their televisions would sometimes turn on by themselves in the middle of the night. No matter what channel the set was tuned to, the show being broadcast was always the same...

Yup. A rerun of—you guessed it—*Little House on the Prairie.*

Bibliography

I read loads of books to bring you this one. Here are a few that stand out.

Baltrusis, Sam. *13 Most Haunted in Massachusetts.* Createspace, 2015.

Balzano, Christopher. *Ghosts of the Bridgewater Triangle.* Atglen, PA: Schiffer Publishing, 2008.

Bowers, Nancy. Iowa Unsolved Murders: Historic Cases.

Edwards, Peter. *Night Justice: The True Story of the Black Donnellys.* Toronto, Canada: Kay Porter Books Ltd., 2004.

Gregory, Ted. Mary Jane's Ghost: The Legacy of a Murder in Small Town America. Iowa City: University of Iowa Press, 2017.

Hunt, Amber and Emily G. Thompson. *Unsolved Murders: True Crime Cases Uncovered.* New York, NY: DK Publishing, 2019.

Lee, Darcy H. *Ghosts of Plymouth, Massachusetts.* Arcadia Publishing, 2017.

Marcus, Scott. *Voices From the Chicago Grave.* Michigan: Thunder Bay Press, 2008.

Mellor, Dr. Lee. Behind the Horror: True Stories That Inspired Horror Movies. New York, NY: Penguin Random House, 2020.

Miller, Orlo. *The Donnellys Must Die.* Toronto, Canada: Macmillan of Canada, 1962.

Norman, Michael and Beth Scott. *Historic Haunted America.* New York, NY: Tom Doherty Associates, 1995.

Ocker, J. W. Cursed Objects: Strange But True Stories of the World's Most Infamous Items. Philadelphia, PA: Quirk Books, 2020.

Patterson, James, with Casey Sherman and Dave Wedge. *The Last Days of John Lennon.* New York, NY: Little, Brown & Co., 2020.

Senger, Deborah Carr. *Haunted Bloomington-Normal, Illinois*. Charleston, SC: Haunted America, 2016.

Shatkins, Candice. *Haunted Kenosha: Ghosts, Legends and Bizarre Tales*. Charleston, SC: Haunted America, 2009.

Shults, Sylvia. *Spirits of Christmas: The Dark Side of the Holidays*. Jacksonville, IL: American Hauntings Ink, 2017.

Taylor, Troy. In the Boneyard: History and Horrors of America's Haunted Cemeteries. Jacksonville, IL: American Hauntings Ink, 2020.

Willis, James. *The Big Book of Ohio Ghost Stories*. Mechanicsburg, PA: Stackpole Books, 2013.

About the Author

Sylvia Shults is the author of *44 Years in Darkness, Fractured Spirits: Hauntings at the Peoria State Hospital*, and other books of true ghost stories. She has spent the past twenty years working in a library, slowly smuggling words out in her pockets day by day to build a book of her own. She sits in dark, spooky, haunted places so you don't have to. She lives a short, ten-minute motorcycle ride away from the haunted asylum that features in so many of her books. She considers it the highest privilege to share the incredible, compassionate history of the Peoria State Hospital.

After battling an intense, lifelong fear of the dark, Sylvia decided to become a ghost hunter. (What WAS she thinking?) As a paranormal investigator, she has made many media appearances, including a tiny part in the Ghost Hunters episode "Prescription for Fear", about the Peoria State Hospital. She is a recurring guest on Ron Hood's podcast *Ron's Amazing Stories*, with the monthly segment "Ghost Stories With Sylvia". She is also the writer, director, producer, and host of the true ghost story podcast Lights Out, available on YouTube, iTunes, iHeart Radio, Spotify, and anywhere else great podcasts are found.

Sylvia loves hearing from her readers, especially when they have spooky stories of their own to share with her. She can be found at www.sylviashults.wordpress.com and on Facebook at the pages for Fractured Spirits and Ghosts of the Illinois River.

Curious about other Crossroad Press books?
Stop by our site:
www.crossroadpress.com
We offer quality writing
in digital, audio, and print formats.